**Edgar Wallace** was born illegitimately in 1875 in Greenwich and adopted by George Freeman, a porter at Billingsgate fish market. At eleven, Wallace sold newspapers at Ludgate Circus and on leaving school took a job with a printer. He enlisted in the Royal West Kent Regiment, later transferring to the Medical Staff Corps, and was sent to South Africa. In 1898 he published a collection of poems called *The Mission that Failed*, left the army and became a correspondent for Reuters.

Wallace became the South African war correspondent for *The Daily Mail*. His articles were later published as *Unofficial Dispatches* and his outspokenness infuriated Kitchener, who banned him as a war correspondent until the First World War. He edited the *Rand Daily Mail*, but gambled disastrously on the South African Stock Market, returning to England to report on crimes and hanging trials. He became editor of *The Evening News*, then in 1905 founded the Tallis Press, publishing *Smithy*, a collection of soldier stories, and *Four Just Men*. At various times he worked on *The Standard*, *The Star*, *The Week-End Racing Supplement* and *The Story Journal*.

In 1917 he became a Special Constable at Lincoln's Inn and also a special interrogator for the War Office. His first marriage to Ivy Caldecott, daughter of a missionary, had ended in divorce and he married his much younger secretary, Violet King.

*The Daily Mail* sent Wallace to investigate atrocities in the Belgian Congo, a trip that provided material for his *Sanders of the River* books. In 1923 he became Chairman of the Press Club and in 1931 stood as a Liberal candidate at Blackpool. On being offered a scriptwriting contract at RKO, Wallace went to Hollywood. He died in 1932, on his way to work on the screenplay for *King Kong*.

THE ADMIRABLE CARFEW

THE ANGEL OF TERROR

THE AVENGER *(USA: THE HAIRY ARM)*

BARBARA ON HER OWN

BIG FOOT

THE BLACK ABBOT

BONES

BONES IN LONDON

BONES OF THE RIVER

THE CLUE OF THE NEW PIN

THE CLUE OF THE SILVER KEY

THE CLUE OF THE TWISTED CANDLE

THE COAT OF ARMS
  *(USA: THE ARRANWAYS MYSTERY)*

THE COUNCIL OF JUSTICE

THE CRIMSON CIRCLE

THE DAFFODIL MYSTERY

THE DARK EYES OF LONDON
  *(USA: THE CROAKERS)*

THE DAUGHTERS OF THE NIGHT

A DEBT DISCHARGED

THE DEVIL MAN

THE DOOR WITH SEVEN LOCKS

THE DUKE IN THE SUBURBS

THE FACE IN THE NIGHT

THE FEATHERED SERPENT

THE FLYING SQUAD

THE FORGER *(USA: THE CLEVER ONE)*

THE FOUR JUST MEN

FOUR SQUARE JANE

THE FOURTH PLAGUE

THE FRIGHTENED LADY

GOOD EVANS

THE HAND OF POWER

THE IRON GRIP

THE JOKER *(USA: THE COLOSSUS)*

THE JUST MEN OF CORDOVA

THE LAW OF THE FOUR JUST MEN

THE LONE HOUSE MYSTERY

THE MAN WHO BOUGHT LONDON

THE MAN WHO KNEW

THE MAN WHO WAS NOBODY

THE MIND OF MR J G REEDER
  *(USA: THE MURDER BOOK
  OF J G REEDER)*

MORE EDUCATED EVANS

MR J G REEDER RETURNS
  *(USA: MR REEDER RETURNS)*

MR JUSTICE MAXELL

RED ACES

ROOM 13

SANDERS

SANDERS OF THE RIVER

THE SINISTER MAN

THE SQUARE EMERALD *(USA: THE
  GIRL FROM SCOTLAND YARD)*

THE THREE JUST MEN

THE THREE OAK MYSTERY

THE TRAITOR'S GATE

WHEN THE GANGS CAME TO
  LONDON

# The Keepers of
# the King's Peace

A "Sanders of the River" book

HOUSE OF
STRATUS

This edition published in 2001 by House of Stratus, an imprint of
House of Stratus Ltd, Thirsk Industrial Park, York Road, Thirsk,
North Yorkshire, YO7 3BX, UK.

www.houseofstratus.com

Typeset by House of Stratus, printed and bound by Short Run Press Limited.

A catalogue record for this book is available from the British Library
and the Library of Congress.

ISBN 1-84232-692-9

We would like to thank the Edgar Wallace Society for all the support they have given
House of Stratus. Enquiries on how to join the Edgar Wallace Society should be addressed to:
The Edgar Wallace Society, c/o Penny Wyrd, 84 Ridgefield Road, Oxford, OX4 3DA.
Email: info@edgarwallace.org  Web: http://www.edgarwallace.org/

# CONTENTS

# BONES, SANDERS AND ANOTHER

To Isongo, which stands upon the tributary of that name, came a woman of the Isisi who had lost her husband through a providential tree falling upon him. I say "providential," for it was notorious that he was an evil man, a drinker of beer and a favourite of many bad persons. Also he made magic in the forest, and was reputedly the familiar of Bashunbi the devil brother of M'shimba-M'shamba. He beat his wives, and once had set fire to his house from sheer wickedness. So that when he was borne back to the village on a grass bier and the women of his house decked themselves with green leaves and arm in arm staggered and stamped through the village street in their death dance, there was a suspicion of hilarity in their song, and a more cheery step in their dance than the occasion called for.

An old man named D'wiri, who knew every step of every dance, saw this and said in his stern way that it was shameless. But he was old and was, moreover, in fear for the decorum of his own obsequies if these outrageous departures from custom were approved or allowed to pass without reprimand.

When M'lama, the wife of G'mami, had seen her lord depart in the canoe for burial in the middle island and had wailed her conventional grief, she washed the dust from her body at the river's edge and went back to her hut. And all that was grief for the dead man was washed away with the dust of mourning.

Many moons came out of the sky, were wasted and died before the woman M'lama showed signs of her gifts. It is said that they appeared one night after a great storm wherein lightning played such strange tricks upon the river that even the old man D'wiri could not remember parallel instances.

In the night the wife of a hunter named E'sani-Osoni brought a dying child into the hut of the widow. He had been choked by a fish-bone and was *in extremis* when M'lama put her hand upon his head and straightway the bone flew from his mouth, "and there was a cry terrible to hear – such a cry as a leopard makes when he is pursued by ghosts."

A week later a baby girl fell into a terrible fit and M'lama had laid her hand upon it and behold! it slept from that moment.

Ahmet, chief of the Government spies, heard of these happenings and came a three days' journey by river to Isongo.

"What are these stories of miracles?" he asked.

"*Capita*," said the chief, using the term of regard which is employed in the Belgian Congo, "this woman M'lama is a true witch and has great gifts, for she raises the dead by the touch of her hand. This I have seen. Also it is said that when U'gomi, the woodcutter, made a fault, cutting his foot in two, this woman healed him marvellously."

"I will see this M'lama," said Ahmet importantly.

He found her in her hut tossing four bones idly. These were the shanks of goats, and each time they fell differently.

"O Ahmet," she said, when he entered, "you have a wife who is sick, also a first-born boy who does not speak though he is more than six seasons old."

Ahmet squatted down by her side.

"Woman," said he, "tell me something that is not the talk of river and I will believe your magic."

"Tomorrow your master, the lord Sandi, will send you a book which will give you happiness," she said.

"Every day my lord sends me a book," retorted the sceptical Ahmet, "and each brings me happiness. Also it is common talk that at this time there come messengers carrying bags of silver and salt to pay men according to their services."

Undismayed she tried her last shot.

"You have a crooked finger which none can straighten – behold!"

She took his hand in hers and pressed the injured phlange. A sharp pain shot up his arm and he winced, pulling back his hand – but the year-old dislocation which had defied the effort of the coast doctor was straightened out, and though the movement was exquisitely painful he could bend it.

"I see you are a true witch," he said, greatly impressed, for a native has a horror of deformity of any kind, and he sent back word of the phenomenon to Sanders.

Sanders at the same time was in receipt of other news which alternately pleased him and filled him with panic. The mail had come in by fast launch and had brought Captain Hamilton of the Houssas a very bulky letter written in a feminine hand. He had broken the glad news to Commissioner Sanders, but that gentleman was not certain in his mind whether the startling intelligence conveyed by the letter was good or bad.

"I'm sure the country will suit her," he said, "this part of the country at any rate – but what will Bones say?"

"Bones!" repeated Captain Hamilton scornfully. "What the dickens does it matter what Bones says?"

Nevertheless, he went to the sea-end of the verandah, and his roar rivalled the thunder of the surf.

"Bones!"

There was no answer and for an excellent reason.

Sanders came out of the bungalow, his helmet on the back of his head, a cheroot tilted dizzily.

"Where is he?" he asked.

Hamilton turned, "I asked him to – at least I didn't ask him, he volunteered – to peg out a trench line."

"Expect an invasion?" asked Saunders.

Hamilton grinned.

"Bones does," he said. "He's full of the idea, and offered to give me tips on the way a trench should be dug – he's feeling rotten about things…you know what I mean. His regiment was at Mons."

Sanders nodded.

"I understand," he said quietly. "And you…you're a jolly good soldier, Hamilton – how do you feel about it all?"

Hamilton shrugged his shoulders.

"They would have taken me for the Cameroons, but somebody had to stay," he said quietly. "After all, it is one's business to…to do one's job in the station of life to which it has pleased God to call him. This is my work…here."

Sanders laid his hand on the other's shoulder.

"That's the game as it should be played," he said, and his blue eyes were as soft and tender as a woman's. "There is no war here – we are the keepers of the King's peace, Hamilton."

"It's rotten…"

"I know – I feel that way myself. We're out of it – the glory of it – the chance of it – the tragedy of it. And there are others. Think of the men in India eating their hearts out…praying for the order that will carry them from the comfort of their lives to the misery and death – and the splendour, I grant you – of war."

He sighed and looked wistfully to the blue sea.

Hamilton beckoned a Houssa corporal who was crossing the garden of the Residency.

"Ho, Mustaf," he said, in his queer coast Arabic, "where shall I look for my lord Tibbetti?"

The corporal turned and pointed to the woods which begin at the back of the Residency and carry without a break for three hundred miles.

"Lord, he went there carrying many strange things – also there went with him Ali Abid, his servant."

Hamilton reached through an open window of the bungalow and fished out his helmet with his walking-stick.

"We'll find Bones," he said grimly; "he's been gone three hours and he's had time to re-plan Verdun."

It took some time to discover the working party, but when it was found the trouble was well repaid.

Bones was stretched on a canvas chair under the shade of a big Isisi palm. His helmet was tipped forward so that the brim rested on the bridge of his nose, his thin red arms were folded on his breast, and their gentle rise and fall testified to his shame. Two pegs had been driven in, and between them a string sagged half-heartedly.

Curled up under a nearby bush was, presumably, Ali Abid – presumably, because all that was visible was a very broad stretch of brown satin skin which showed between the waistline of a pair of white cotton trousers and a duck jacket.

They looked down at the unconscious Bones for a long time in silence.

"What will he say when I kick him?" asked Hamilton. "You can have the first guess."

Sanders frowned thoughtfully.

"He'll say that he was thinking out a new system of communicating trenches," he said. "He's been boring me to tears over saps and things."

Hamilton shook his head.

"Wrong, sir," he said; "that isn't the lie he'll tell. He will say that I kept him up so late last night working at the men's pay-sheets that he couldn't keep awake."

Bones slept on.

"He may say that it was coffee after tiffin," suggested Sanders after a while; "he said the other day that coffee always made him sleep."

" 'Swoon' was the word he used, sir," corrected Hamilton. "I don't think he'll offer that suggestion now – the only other excuse I can think of is that he was repeating the Bomongo irregular verbs. Bones!"

He stooped and broke off a long grass and inserted it in the right ear of Lieutenant Tibbetts, twiddling the end delicately. Bones made a feeble clutch at his ear, but did not open his eyes.

"Bones!" said Hamilton, and kicked him less gently. "Get up, you lazy devil – there's an invasion."

Bones leapt to his feet and staggered a little; blinked fiercely at his superior and saluted.

"Enemy on the left flank, sir," he reported stiffly. "Shall we have dinner or take a taxi?"

"Wake up, Napoleon," begged Hamilton, "you're at Waterloo."

Bones blinked more slowly.

"I'm afraid I've been unconscious, dear old officer," he confessed. "The fact is – "

"Listen to this, everybody," said Hamilton admiringly.

"The fact is, sir," said Bones, with dignity, "I fell asleep – that beastly coffee I had after lunch, added to the fatigue of sittin' up half the night with those jolly old accounts of yours, got the better of me. I was sittin' down workin' out one of the dinkiest little ideas in trenches – a sort of communicating trench where you needn't get wet in the rainiest weather – when I – well, I just swooned off."

Hamilton looked disappointed.

"Weren't you doing anything with the Bomongo verbs?" he demanded.

A light came to Bones' eyes.

"By Jove, sir!" he said heartily, "that was it, of course... The last thing I remember was..."

"Kick that man of yours and come back to the bungalow," Hamilton interrupted, "there's a job for you, my boy."

He walked across and stirred the second sleeper with the toe of his boot.

Ali Abid wriggled round and sat up.

He was square of face, with a large mouth and two very big brown eyes. He was enormously fat, but it was not fat of the flabby type. Though he called himself Ali, it was, as Bones admitted, "sheer swank" to do so, for this man had "coast" written all over him.

He got up slowly and saluted first his master, then Sanders, and lastly Hamilton.

Bones had found him at Cape Coast Castle on the occasion of a joy-ride which the young officer had taken on a British man-of-war. Ali Abid had been the heaven-sent servant, and though Sanders had a horror of natives who spoke English, the English of Ali Abid was his very own.

He had been for five years the servant of Professor Garrileigh, the eminent bacteriologist, the account of whose researches in the field of tropical medicines fill eight volumes of closely printed matter, every page of which contains words which are not to be found in most lexicons.

They walked back to the Residency, Ali Abid in the rear.

"I want you to go up to the Isongo, Bones," said Sanders; "there may be some trouble there – a woman is working miracles."

"He may get a new head," murmured Hamilton, but Bones pretended not to hear.

"Use your tact and get back before the 17th for the party."

"The – ?" asked Bones.

He had an irritating trick of employing extravagant gestures of a fairly commonplace kind. Thus, if he desired to hear a statement repeated – though he had heard it well enough the first time – he would bend his head with a puzzled wrinkle of forehead, put his hand to his ear and wait anxiously, even painfully, for the repetition.

"You heard what the Commissioner said," growled Hamilton. "Party – P-A-R-T-Y."

"My birthday is not until April, your Excellency," said Bones.

"I'd guess the date – but what's the use?" interposed Hamilton.

"It isn't a birthday party, Bones," said Sanders. "We are giving a house-warming for Miss Hamilton."

Bones gasped, and turned an incredulous eye upon his chief. "You haven't a sister, surely, dear old officer?" he asked.

"Why the dickens shouldn't I have a sister?" demanded his chief.

Bones shrugged his shoulders.

"A matter of deduction, sir," he said quietly. "Absence of all evidence of a soothin' and lovin' influence in your lonely and unsympathetic upbringin'; hardness of heart an' a disposition to nag, combined with a rough and unpromisin' exterior – a sister, good Lord!"

"Anyway, she's coming, Bones," said Hamilton; "and she's looking forward to seeing you – I've written an awful lot about you."

Bones smirked.

"Of course," he said, "you've overdone it a bit – women hate to be disillusioned. What you ought to have done, sir, is to describe me as a

7

sort of ass – genial and all that sort of thing, but a commonplace sort of ass."

Hamilton nodded.

"That's exactly what I've done, Bones," he said. "I told her how Bosambo did you in the eye for twenty pounds, and how you fell into the water looking for buried treasure, and how the Isisi tried to sell you a flying crocodile and would have sold it too, if it hadn't been for my timely arrival. I told her – "

"I think you've said enough, sir."

Bones was very red and very haughty.

"Far be it from me to resent your attitude or contradict your calumnies. Miss Hamilton will see very little of me. An inflexible sense of duty will keep me away from the frivolous circle of society, sir. Alert an' sleepless – "

"Trenches," said Hamilton brutally.

Bones winced, regarded his superior for a moment with pain, saluted, and turning on his heel, stalked away, followed by Ali Abid no less pained.

He left at dawn the next morning, and both Sanders and Hamilton came down to the concrete quay to see the *Zaire* start on her journey. Sanders gave his final instructions – "If the woman is upsetting the people, arrest her; if she has too big a hold on them, arrest her; but if she is just amusing them, come back."

"And don't forget the 17th," said Hamilton.

"I may arrive a little late for that," said Bones gravely." I don't wish to be a skeleton at your jolly old festive board, dear old sportsman – you will excuse my absence to Miss Hamilton. I shall probably have a headache and all that sort of thing."

He waved a sad farewell as the *Zaire* passed round the bend of the river, and looked, as he desired to look, a melancholy figure with his huge pipe in his mouth and his hands thrust dejectedly into his trousers pockets.

Once out of sight he became his own jovial self.

"Lieutenant Ali," he said, "get out my log and put it in old Sanders' cabin, make me a cup of tea and keep her jolly old head east, east by north."

"Ay, ay, sir," said Ali in excellent English.

The "log" which Bones kept was one of the secret documents which never come under the eye of the superior authorities. There were such entries as –

Wind NNW. Sea calm. Hostile craft sighted on port bow, at 10.31 a.m. General Quarters sounded 10.32. Interrogated Captain of the hostile craft and warned him not to fish in fairway. Sighted Cape M'Gooboori 12.17, stopped for lunch and wood.

What though Cape M'Gooboori was the village of that name and the "calm sea" was no more than the placid bosom of the Great River? What though Bones' "hostile craft" was a dilapidated canoe, manned by one aged and bewildered man of the Isisi engaged in spearing fish? Bones saw all things through the rosy spectacles of adventurous youth denied its proper share of experience.

At sunset the *Zaire* came gingerly through the shoals that run out from the Isongo beach, and Bones went ashore to conduct his investigations. It chanced that the evening had been chosen by M'lama, the witch, for certain wonderful manifestations, and the village was almost deserted.

In a wood and in a place of green trees M'lama sat tossing her sheep shanks, and a dense throng of solemn men and women squatted or sat or tiptoed about her – leaving her a respectable space for her operations. A bright fire crackled and glowed at her side, and into this, from time to time, she thrust little sticks of plaited straw and drew them forth blazing and spluttering until with a quick breath she extinguished the flame and examined the grey ash.

"Listen, all people," she said, "and be silent, lest my great ju-ju strike you dead. What man gave me this?"

"It was I, M'lama," said an eager woman, her face wrinkled with apprehension as she held up her brown palm.

The witch peered forward at the speaker.

"O F'sela!" she chanted, "there is a man-child for thee who shall be greater than chiefs; also you will suffer from a sickness which shall make you mad."

"O ko!"

Half dismayed by the promise of her own fate; half exalted by the career the witch had sketched for her unborn son, the woman stared incredulously, fearfully at the swaying figure by the fire.

Again a plaited stick went into the fire, was withdrawn and blown out, and the woman again prophesied.

And sometimes it was of honours and riches she spoke, and sometimes – and more often – of death and disaster. Into this shuddering group strode Bones, very finely clad in white raiment yet limp withal, for the night was close and the way had been long and rough.

The sitters scrambled to their feet, their knuckles at their teeth, for this was a moment of great embarrassment.

"Oh M'lama," said Bones agreeably, and spoke in the soft dialect of the Isisi by-the-river, "prophesy for me!"

She looked up sullenly, divining trouble for herself.

"Lord," she said, with a certain smooth venom, "there is a great sickness for you – and behold you will go far away and die, and none shall miss you."

Bones went very red, shook an indignant forefinger at the offending prophetess.

"You're a wicked old storyteller!" he stammered. "You're depressin' the people – you naughty girl! I hate you – I simply loathe you!"

As he spoke in English she was not impressed.

"Goin' about the country puttin' people off their grub, by Jove!" he stormed; "tellin' stories...oh dash it, I shall have to be awfully severe with you!"

Severe he was, for he arrested her, to the relief of her audience, who waited long enough to discover whether or not her ju-ju would strike him dead, and being obviously disappointed by her failure to provide this spectacle, melted away.

Close to the gangway of the *Zaire* she persuaded one of her Houssa guard to release his hold. She persuaded him by the simple expedient of burying her sharp white teeth in the fleshy part of his arm – and bolted. They captured her half mad with panic and fear of her unknown fate, and brought her to the boat.

Bones, fussing about the struggling group, dancing with excitement, was honourably wounded by the chance contact of his nose with a wild and whirling fist.

"Put her in the store cabin!" he commanded breathlessly. "Oh, what a wicked woman!"

In the morning as the boat got under way Ali came to him with a distressing story.

"Your Excellency will be pained to hear," he said, "that the female prisoner has eradicated her costume."

"Eradicated…?" repeated the puzzled Bones, gently touching the patch of sticking-plaster on his nose.

"In the night," explained this former slave of science, "the subject has developed symptoms of mania, and has entirely dispensed with her clothes – to wit, by destruction."

"She's torn up her clothes?" gasped Bones, his hair rising, and Ali nodded.

Now, the dress of a native woman varies according to the degree in which she falls under missionary influence. Isongo was well within the sphere of the River Mission, and so M'lama's costume consisted of a tight-fitting piece of print which wound round and round the body in the manner of a kilt, covering the figure from armpit to feet.

Bones went to the open window of the prison cabin, and steadfastly averting his gaze, called –

"M'lama!"

No reply came, and he called again.

"M'lama," he said gently, in the river dialect, "what shall Sandi say to this evil that you do?"

There was no reply, only a snuffling sound of woe.

"Oh, ai!" sobbed the voice.

"M'lama, presently we shall come to the Mission house where the God-men are, and I will bring you clothing – these you will put on you," said Bones, still staring blankly over the side of the ship at the waters which foamed past her low hull; for if my lord Sandi see you as I see you – I mean as I wouldn't for the world see you, you improper person," he corrected himself hastily in English – "if my lord Sandi saw you, he would feel great shame. Also," he added, as a horrible thought made him go cold all over, "also the lady who comes to my lord Militini – oh lor!"

These last two words were in English.

Fortunately there was a Jesuit settlement near by, and here Bones stopped and interviewed the stout and genial priest in charge.

"It's curious how they all do it," reflected the priest, as he led the way to his storehouse. "I've known 'em to tear up their clothes in an East End police cell – white folk, the same as you and I."

He rummaged in a big box and produced certain garments. "My last consignment from a well-meaning London congregation," he smiled, and flung out a heap of dresses, hats, stockings and shoes. "If they'd sent a roll or two of print I might have used them – but strong religious convictions do not entirely harmonize with a last year's Paris model."

Bones, flushed and unhappy, grabbed an armful of clothing, and showering the chuckling priest with an incoherent medley of apology and thanks, hurried back to the *Zaire.*

"Behold, M'lama," he said, as he thrust his loot through the window of the little deck-house, "there are many grand things such as great ladies wear – now you shall appear before Sandi beautiful to see."

He logged the happening in characteristic language, and was in the midst of this literary exercise when the tiny steamer charged a sandbank, and before her engines could slow or reverse she had slid to the top and rested in two feet of water.

A rueful Bones surveyed the situation and returned to his cabin to conclude his diary with –

12.19 struck a reef off B'lidi Bay. Fear vessel total wreck. Boats all ready for lowering.

As a matter of fact there were neither boats to lower nor need to lower them, because the crew were already standing in the river (up to their hips) and were endeavouring to push the *Zaire* to deep water.

In this they were unsuccessful, and it was not for thirty-six hours until the river, swollen by heavy rains in the Ochori region, lifted the *Zaire* clear of the obstruction, that Bones might record the story of his salvage.

He had released a reformed M'lama to the greater freedom of the deck, and save for a shrill passage at arms between that lady and the corporal she had bitten, there was no sign of a return to her evil ways. She wore a white pique skirt and a white blouse, and on her head she balanced deftly, without the aid of pins, a yellow straw hat with long trailing ribbons of heliotrope. Alternately they trailed behind and before.

"A horrible sight," said Bones, shuddering at his first glimpse of her.

The rest of the journey was uneventful until the *Zaire* had reached the northernmost limits of the Residency reserve. Sanders had partly cleared and wholly drained four square miles of the little peninsula on which the Residency stood, and by barbed wire and deep cutting had isolated the government estate from the wild forest land to the north.

Here, the river shoals in the centre, cutting a passage to the sea through two almost unfathomable channels close to the eastern and western banks. Bones had locked away his journal and was standing on the bridge rehearsing the narrative which was to impress his superiors with a sense of his resourcefulness – and incidentally present himself in the most favourable light to the new factor which was coming into his daily life.

He had thought of Hamilton's sister at odd intervals and now...

The *Zaire* was hugging the western bank so closely that a bold and agile person might have stepped ashore.

M'lama, the witch, was both bold and agile.

He turned with open mouth to see something white and feminine leap the space between deck and shore, two heliotrope ribbons streaming wildly in such breeze as there was.

"Hi! Don't do that...naughty, naughty!" yelled the agonized Bones, but she had disappeared into the undergrowth before the big paddle-wheel of the *Zaire* began to thresh madly astern.

Never was the resourcefulness of Bones more strikingly exemplified. An ordinary man would have leapt overboard in pursuit, but Bones was no ordinary man. He remembered in that moment of crisis, the distressing propensity of his prisoner to the "eradication of garments." With one stride he was in his cabin and had snatched a counterpane from his bed, in two bounds he was over the rail on the bank and running swiftly in the direction the fugitive had taken.

For a little time he did not see her, then he glimpsed the white of a pique dress, and with a yell of admonition started in pursuit.

She stood hesitating a moment, then fled, but he was on her before she had gone a dozen yards; the counterpane was flung over her head, and though she kicked and struggled and indulged in muffled squeaks, he lifted her up in his arms and staggered back to the boat.

They ran out a gangway plank and across this he passed with his burden, declining all offers of assistance.

"Close the window," he gasped; "open the door – now, you naughty old lady!"

He bundled her in, counterpane enmeshed and reduced to helpless silence, slammed the door and leant panting against the cabin, mopping his brow.

"Phew!" said Bones, and repeated the inelegant remark many times. All this happened almost within sight of the quay on which Sanders and Hamilton were waiting. It was a very important young man who saluted them.

"All correct, sir," said Bones, stiff as a ramrod; "no casualties – except as per my nose which will be noted in the margin of my report – one female prisoner secured after heroic chase, which, I trust, sir, you will duly report to my jolly old superiors – "

"Don't gas so much, Bones," said Hamilton. "Come along and meet my sister – hullo, what the devil's that?"

They turned with one accord to the forest path.

Two native policemen were coming towards them, and between them a bedraggled M'lama, her skirt all awry, her fine hat at a rakish angle, stepped defiantly.

"Heavens!" said Bones, "she's got away again… That's my prisoner, dear old officer!"

Hamilton frowned.

"I hope she hasn't frightened Pat…she was walking in the reservation."

Bones did not faint, his knees went from under him, but he recovered by clutching the arm of his faithful Ali.

"Dear old friend," he murmured brokenly, "accidents…error of judgment…the greatest tragedy of my life…"

"What's the matter with you?" demanded Sanders in alarm, for the face of Bones was ghastly.

Lieutenant Tibbetts made no reply, but walked with unsteady steps to the lock-up, fumbled with the key and opened the door.

There stepped forth a dishevelled and wrathful girl (she was a little scared, too, I suspect), the most radiant and lovely figure that had ever dawned on the horizon of Bones.

She looked from her staggered brother to Sanders, from Sanders to her miserable custodian.

"What on earth – " began Hamilton.

Then her lips twitched and she fell into a fit of uncontrollable laughter.

"If," said Bones huskily, "if in an excess of zeal I mistook…in the gloamin', madame…white dress…"

He spread out his arms in a gesture of extravagant despair. "I can do no more than a gentleman… I have a loaded revolver in my cabin…farewell!"

He bowed deeply to the girl, saluted his dumbfounded chief, tripped up over a bucket and would have fallen but for Hamilton's hand.

15

"You're an ass," said Hamilton, struggling to preserve his sense of annoyance. "Pat – this is Lieutenant Tibbetts, of whom I have often written."

The girl looked at Bones, her eyes moist with laughter.

"I guessed it from the first," she said, and Bones writhed.

# BONES CHANGES HIS RELIGION

Captain Hamilton of the King's Houssas had two responsibilities in life, a sister and a subaltern.

The sister's name was Patricia Agatha, the subaltern had been born Tibbetts, christened Augustus, and named by Hamilton in his arbitrary way, "Bones."

Whilst sister and subaltern were separated from one another by some three thousand miles of ocean – as far, in fact, as the Coast is from Bradlesham Thorpe in the County of Hampshire – Captain Hamilton bore his responsibilities without displaying a sense of the burden.

When Patricia Hamilton decided on paying a visit to her brother she did so with his heartiest approval, for he did not realize that in bringing his two responsibilities face to face he was not only laying the foundation of serious trouble, but was actually engaged in erecting the fabric.

Pat Hamilton had come and had been boisterously welcomed by her brother one white-hot morning, Houssas in undress uniform lining the beach and gazing solemnly upon Militini's riotous joy. Mr Commissioner Sanders, CMG, had given her a more formal welcome, for he was a little scared of women. Bones, as we know, had not been present – which was unfortunate in more ways than one.

It made matters no easier for the wretched Bones that Miss Hamilton was an exceedingly lovely lady. Men who lived for a long time in native lands and see little save beautiful figures displayed without art and with very little adornment, are apt to regard any white woman with regular features as pretty, when the vision comes to them after a long interval spent amidst native people. But it needed neither contrast nor comparison to induce an admiration for Captain Hamilton's sister.

She was of a certain Celtic type, above the medium height, with the freedom of carriage and gait which is the peculiar possession of her countrywomen. Her face was a true oval, and her complexion of that kind which tans readily but does not freckle.

Eyes and mouth were firm and steadfast; she was made for ready laughter, yet she was deep enough, and in eyes and mouth alike you read a tenderness beyond disguise. She had a trinity of admirers: her brother's admiration was natural and critical; Sanders admired and feared; Lieutenant Tibbetts admired and resented.

From the moment when Bones strode off after the painful discovery, had slammed the door of his hut and had steadfastly declined all manner of food and sustenance, he had voluntarily cut himself off from his kind.

He met Hamilton on parade the following morning, hollow-eyed (as he hoped) after a sleepless night, and there was nothing in his attitude suggestive of the deepest respect and the profoundest regard for that paragraph of King's Regulations which imposes upon the junior officer a becoming attitude of humility in the presence of his superior officer.

"How is your head, Bones?" asked Hamilton, after the parade had been dismissed.

"Thank you, sir," said Bones bitterly – though why he should be bitter at the kindly inquiry only he knew – "thank you sir, it is about the same. My temperature is – or was – up to one hundred and four, and I have been delirious. I wouldn't like to say, dear old – sir, that I'm not nearly delirious now."

"Come up to tiffin," invited Hamilton.

Bones saluted – a sure preliminary to a dramatic oration. "Sir," he said firmly, "you've always been a jolly old officer to me before this contretemps wrecked my young life – but I shall never be quite the same man again, sir."

"Don't be an ass," begged Hamilton.

"Revile me, sir," said Bones dismally; "give me a dangerous mission, one of those jolly old adventures where a feller takes his life in one hand, his revolver in the other, but don't ask me – "

"My sister wants to see you," said Hamilton, cutting short the flow of eloquence.

"Ha, ha!" laughed Bones hollowly, and strode into his hut.

"And what I'm going to do with him, Heaven knows," groaned Hamilton at tiffin. "The fact is, Pat, your arrival on the scene has thoroughly demoralized him."

The girl folded her serviette and walked to the window, and stood looking out over the yellow stretch of the deserted parade-ground.

"I'm going to call on Bones," she said suddenly.

"Poor Bones!" murmured Sanders.

"That's very rude!" She took down her solar helmet from the peg behind the door and adjusted it carefully. Then she stepped through the open door, whistling cheerfully.

"I hope you don't mind, sir," apologized Hamilton, "but we've never succeeded in stopping her habit of whistling."

Sanders laughed.

"It would be strange if she didn't whistle," he said cryptically.

Bones was lying on his back, his hands behind his head. A half-emptied tin of biscuits, no less than the remnants of a box of chocolates, indicated that anchorite as he was determined to be, his austerity did not run in the direction of starvation.

His mind was greatly occupied by a cinematograph procession of melancholy pictures. Perhaps he would go away, far, far, into the interior. Even into the territory of the great king where a man's life is worth about five cents net. And as day by day passed and no news came of him – as how could it when his habitation was marked by a cairn of stones? – she would grow anxious and unhappy. And presently messengers would come bringing her a few poor trinkets he had bequeathed to her – a wrist-watch, a broken sword, a silver cigarette-case dented with the arrow that slew him – and she would weep silently in the loneliness of her room.

19

And perhaps he would find strength to send a few scrawled words asking for her pardon, and the tears would well up in her beautiful grey eyes – as they were already welling in Bones' eyes at the picture he drew – and she would know – all.

"Phweet!"

Or else, maybe he would be stricken down with fever, and she would want to come and nurse him, but he would refuse.

"Tell her," he would say weakly, but oh, so bravely, "tell her…I ask only…her pardon."

"Phweet!"

Bones heard the second whistle. It came from the open window immediately above his head. A song bird was a rare visitor to these parts, but he was too lazy and too absorbed to look up.

Perhaps (he resumed) she would never see him again, never know the deep sense of injustice…

"Phwee – et!"

It was clearer and more emphatic, and he half turned his head to look –

He was on his feet in a second, his hand raised to his damp forehead, for leaning on the window sill, her lips pursed for yet another whistle, was the lady of his thoughts.

She met his eyes sternly.

"Come outside – misery!" she said, and Bones gasped and obeyed.

"What do you mean," she demanded, "by sulking in your wretched little hut when you ought to be crawling about on your hands and knees begging my pardon?"

Bones said nothing.

"Bones," said this outrageous girl, shaking her head reprovingly, "you want a jolly good slapping!"

Bones extended his bony wrist.

"Slap!" he said defiantly.

He had hardly issued the challenge when a very firm young palm, driven by an arm toughened by long acquaintance with the royal and ancient game, came "Smack!" and Bones winced.

"Play the game, dear old Miss Hamilton," he said, rubbing his wrist.

"Play the game yourself, dear old Bones," she mimicked him. "You ought to be ashamed of yourself – "

"Let bygones be bygones, jolly old Miss Hamilton," begged Bones magnanimously. "And now that I see you're a sport, put it there, if it weighs a ton."

And he held out his nobbly hand and caught the girl's in a grip that made her grimace.

Five minutes later he was walking her round the married quarters of his Houssas, telling her the story of his earliest love affair. She was an excellent listener, and seldom interrupted him save to ask if there was any insanity in his family, or whether the girl was short-sighted; in fact, as Bones afterwards said, it might have been Hamilton himself.

"What on earth are they finding to talk about?" wondered Sanders, watching the confidences from the depths of a big cane chair on the verandah.

"Bones," replied Hamilton lazily, "is telling her the story of his life and how he saved the territories from rebellion. He's also begging her not to breathe a word of this to me for fear of hurting my feelings."

At that precise moment Bones was winding up a most immodest recital of his accomplishments with a less immodest footnote.

"Of course, dear old Miss Hamilton," he was saying, lowering his voice, "I shouldn't like a word of this to come to your jolly old brother's ears. He's an awfully good sort, but naturally in competition with an agile mind like mine, understanding the native as I do, he hasn't an earthly – "

"Why don't you write the story of your adventures?" she asked innocently. "It would sell like hot cakes."

Bones choked with gratification.

"Precisely my idea – oh, what a mind you've got! What a pity it doesn't run in the family! I'll tell you a precious secret – not a word to anybody – honest?"

"Honest," she affirmed.

Bones looked round.

"It's practically ready for the publisher," he whispered, and stepped back to observe the effect of his words.

She shook her head in admiration, her eyes were dancing with delight, and Bones realized that here at last he had met a kindred soul.

"It must be awfully interesting to write books," she sighed. "I've tried – but can never invent anything."

"Of course, in my case – " corrected Bones.

"I suppose you just sit down with a pen in your hand and imagine all sorts of things," she mused, directing her feet to the Residency.

"This is the story of my life," explained Bones earnestly. "Not fiction…but all sorts of adventures that actually happened."

"To whom?" she asked.

"To me," claimed Bones, louder than was necessary.

"Oh!" she said.

"Don't start 'Oh-ing,' " said Bones in a huff. "If you and I are going to be good friends, dear old Miss Hamilton, don't say 'Oh!' "

"Don't be a bully, Bones." She turned on him so fiercely that he shrank back.

"Play the game," he said feebly; "play the game, dear old sister!"

She led him captive to the stoep and deposited him in the easiest chair she could find.

From that day he ceased to be anything but a slave, except on one point.

The question of missions came up at tiffin, and Miss Hamilton revealed the fact that she favoured the High Church and held definite views on the clergy.

Bones confessed that he was a Wesleyan.

"Do you mean to tell me that you're a Nonconformist?" she asked incredulously.

"That's my dinky little religion, dear old Miss Hamilton," said Bones. "I'd have gone into the Church only I hadn't enough – enough – "

"Brains?" suggested Hamilton.

"Call is the word," said Bones. "I wasn't called – or if I was I was out – haw-haw! That's a rippin' little bit of persiflage, Miss Hamilton?"

"Be serious, Bones," said the girl; "you musn't joke about things."

She put him through a cross-examination to discover the extent of his convictions. In self-defence Bones, with only the haziest idea of the doctrine he defended, summarily dismissed certain of Miss Hamilton's most precious beliefs.

"But, Bones," she persisted, "if I asked you to change – "

Bones shook his head.

"Dear old friend," he said solemnly, "there are two things I'll never do – alter the faith of my distant but happy youth, or listen to one disparagin' word about the jolliest old sister that ever – "

"That will do, Bones," she said, with dignity. "I can see that you don't like me as I thought you did – what do you think, Mr Sanders?"

Sanders smiled.

"I can hardly judge – you see," he added apologetically, "I'm a Wesleyan too."

"Oh!" said Patricia, and fled in confusion.

Bones rose in silence, crossed to his chief and held out his hand.

"Brother," he said brokenly.

"What the devil are you doing?" snarled Sanders.

"Spoken like a true Christian, dear old Excellency and sir," murmured Bones. "We'll bring her back to the fold."

He stepped nimbly to the door, and the serviette ring that Sanders threw with unerring aim caught his angular shoulder as he vanished.

That same night Sanders had joyful news to impart. He came into the Residency to find Bones engaged in mastering the art of embroidery under the girl's tuition.

Sanders interrupted what promised to be a most artistic execution.

"Who says a joy-ride to the upper waters of the Isisi?"

Hamilton jumped up.

"Joy-ride?" he said, puzzled.

Sanders nodded.

"We leave tomorrow for the Lesser Isisi to settle a religious palaver – Bucongo of the Lesser Isisi is getting a little too enthusiastic a Christian, and Ahmet has been sending some queer reports. I've been putting off the palaver for weeks, but Administration says it has no objection to my making a picnic of duty – so we'll all go."

"Tri-umph!" said Hamilton. "Bones, leave your needlework and go overhaul the stores."

Bones, kneeling on a chair, his elbows on the table, looked up.

"As jolly old Francis Drake said when the Spanish Armada – "

"To the stores, you insubordinate beggar!" commanded Hamilton, and Bones made a hurried exit.

The accommodation of the *Zaire* was limited, but there was the launch, a light-draught boat which was seldom used except for tributary work.

"I could put Bones in charge of the *Wiggle*," he said, "but he'd be pretty sure to smash her up. Miss Hamilton will have my cabin, and you and I could take the two smaller cabins."

Bones, to whom it was put, leapt at the suggestion, brushing aside all objections. They were answered before they were framed.

As for the girl, she was beside herself with joy.

"Will there be any fighting?" she asked breathlessly. "Shall we be attacked?"

Sanders shook his head smilingly.

"All you have to do," said Bones confidently, "is to stick to me. Put your faith in old Bones. When you see the battle swayin' an' it isn't certain which way it's goin', look for my jolly old banner wavin' above the stricken field."

"And be sure it *is* his banner," interrupted Hamilton, "and not his large feet. Now the last time we had a fight…"

And he proceeded to publish and utter a scandalous libel, Bones protesting incoherently the while.

The expedition was on the point of starting when Hamilton took his junior aside.

"Bones," he said, not unkindly, "I know you're a whale of a navigator, and all that sort of thing, and my sister, who has an awfully keen sense of humour, would dearly love to see you at the helm of the *Wiggle*, but as the Commissioner wants to make a holiday, I think it would be best if you left the steering to one of the boys."

Bones drew himself up stiffly.

"Dear old officer," he said aggrieved, "I cannot think that you wish to speak disparagingly of my intelligence – "

"Get that silly idea out of your head," said Hamilton. "That is just what I'm trying to do."

"I'm under your jolly old orders, sir," Bones said with the air of an early Christian martyr, "and according to Paragraph 156 of King's Regulations – "

"Don't let us go into that," said Hamilton. "I'm not giving you any commands, I'm merely making a sensible suggestion. Of course, if you want to make an ass of yourself – "

"I have never had the slightest inclination that way, cheery old sir," said Bones, "and I'm not likely at my time of life to be influenced by my surroundings."

He saluted again and made his way to the barracks. Bones had a difficulty in packing his stores. In truth they had all been packed before he reached the *Wiggle*, and to an unprofessional eye they were packed very well indeed, but Bones had them turned out and packed *his* way. When that was done, and it was obvious to the meanest intelligence that the *Wiggle* was in terrible danger of capsizing before she started, the stores were unshipped and rearranged under the directions of the fuming Hamilton.

When the third packing was completed, the general effect bore a striking resemblance to the position of the stores as Bones had found them when he came to the boat. When everybody was ready to start, Bones remembered that he had forgotten his log-book, and there was another wait.

"Have you got everything now?" asked Sanders wearily, leaning over the rail.

"Everything, sir," said Bones, with a salute to his superior, and a smile to the girl.

"Have you got your hot-water bottle and your haircurlers?" demanded Hamilton offensively.

Bones favoured him with a dignified stare, made a signal to the engineer, and the *Wiggle* started forward, as was her wont, with a jerk which put upon Bones the alternative of making a most undignified sprawl or clutching a very hot smoke-stack. He chose the latter, recovered his balance with an easy grace, punctiliously saluted the tiny flag of the *Zaire* as he whizzed past her, and under the very eyes of Hamilton, with all the calmness in the world, took the wheel from the steersman's hand and ran the *Wiggle* ashore.

All this he did in the brief space of three minutes.

"And," said Hamilton, exasperated to a degree, "if you'd only broken your infernal head, the accident would have been worth it."

It took half an hour for the *Wiggle* to get afloat again. She had run up the beach, and it was necessary to unload the stores, carry them back to the quay and reload her again.

"*Now* are you ready?" said Sanders.

"Ay, ay, sir," said Bones, abased but nautical.

Bucongo, the chief of the Lesser Isisi folk, had a dispute with his brother-in-law touching a certain matter which affected his honour. It affected his life eventually, since his relative was found one morning dead of a spear-thrust. This Sanders discovered after the big trial which followed certain events described hereafter.

The brother-in-law in his malice had sworn that Bucongo held communion with devils. It is a fact that Bucongo had, at an early age, been captured by Catholic missionaries, and had spent an uncomfortable youth mastering certain mysterious rites and ceremonies. His brother-in-law had been in the blessed service of another missionary who taught that God lived in the river, and that to fully benefit by his ju-ju it was necessary to be immersed in the flowing stream.

Between the water-God men and the cross-God men there was ever a feud, each speaking disparagingly of the other, though converts to each creed had this in common, that neither understood completely the faith into which they were newly admitted. The advantage lay with the Catholic converts because they were given a pewter medal with hearts and sun like radiations engraved thereon (this medal was admittedly a cure for toothache and pains in the stomach), whilst the Protestants had little beyond a mysterious something that they referred to as A'lamo – which means Grace.

But when taunted by their medal-flaunting rivals and challenged to produce this "Grace," they were crestfallen and ashamed, being obliged to admit that A'lamo was an invisible magic which (they stoutly affirmed) was nevertheless an excellent magic, since it preserved one from drowning and cured warts and boils.

Bucongo, the most vigorous partisan of the cross-God men, and an innovator of ritual, found amusement in watching the Baptist missionaries standing knee-deep in the river washing the souls of the converts.

He had even been insolent to young Ferguson, the earnest leader of the American Baptist Mission, and to his intense amazement had been suddenly floored with a left-hander delivered by the sometime Harvard middle weight.

He carried his grievance and a lump on his jaw to Mr Commissioner Sanders, who had arrived at the junction of the Isisi and the N'gomi rivers and was holding his palaver, and Sanders had been unsympathetic.

"Go worship your God in peace," said Sanders, "and let all other men worship theirs; and say no evil word to white men for these are very quick to anger. Also it is unbecoming that a black man should speak scornfully to his masters."

"Lord," said Bucongo, "in heaven all men are as one, black or white."

"In heaven," said Sanders, "we will settle that palaver, but here on the river we hold our places by our merits. Tomorrow I come to your village to inquire into certain practices of which the God-men know nothing – this palaver is finished."

Now Bucongo was something more than a convert. He was a man of singular intelligence and of surprising originality. He had been a lay missioner of the Church, and had made many converts to a curious religion, the ritual of which was only half revealed to the good Jesuit fathers when at a great palaver which Bucongo summoned to exhibit his converts, the Church service was interspersed with the sacrifice of

27

a goat and a weird procession and dance which left the representative of The Order speechless. Bucongo was called before a conference of the Mission and reprimanded.

He offered excuses, but there was sufficient evidence to prove that this enthusiastic Christian had gone systematically to work, to found, what amounted to a religion of his own.

The position was a little delicate, and any other Order than the Jesuits might have hesitated to tackle a reform which meant losing a very large membership.

The fate of Bucongo's congregation had been decided when, in his anger, he took canoe, and travelling for half a day, came to the principal Mission.

Father Carpentier, full-bearded, red of face and brawny of arm, listened in the shade of his hut, pulling thoughtfully at a long pipe.

"And so, Pentini," concluded Bucongo, "even Sandi puts shame on me because I am a cross-God man, and he by all accounts is of the water-God ju-ju."

The father eyed this perturbed sheep of his flock thoughtfully.

"O Bucongo," he said gently, "in the river lands are many beasts. Those which fly and which swim; those that run swiftly and that hide in the earth. Now who of these is right?"

"Lord, they are all right but are of different ways," said Bucongo.

Father Carpentier nodded.

"Also in the forest are two ants – one who lives in tree nests, and one who has a home deep in the ground. They are of a kind, and have the same business. Yet God put it into the little heads of one to climb trees, and of the other to burrow deeply. Both are right and neither are wrong, save when the tree ant meets the ground ant and fights him. Then both are wrong."

The squatting Bucongo rose sullenly.

"Master," he said, "these mysteries are too much for a poor man. I think I know a better ju-ju, and to him I go."

"You have no long journey, Chief," said the father sternly, "for they tell me stories of ghost dances in the forest and a certain Bucongo who is the leader of these – and of a human sacrifice. Also of converts who are branded with a cross of hot iron."

The chief looked at his sometime tutor with face twisted and puckered with rage, and turning without a word, walked back to his canoe.

The next morning Father Carpentier sent a messenger to Sanders bearing an urgent letter, and Sanders read the closely written lines with a troubled frown.

He put down the letter and came out on to the deck, to find Hamilton fishing over the side of the steamer. Hamilton looked round.

"Anything wrong?" he asked quickly.

"Bucongo of the Lesser Isisi is wrong," said Sanders. "I have heard of his religious meetings and have been a little worried – there will be a big ju-ju palaver or I'm very much mistaken. Where is Bones?"

"He has taken my sister up the creek – Bones says there are any number of egrets' nests there, and I believe he is right."

Sanders frowned again.

"Send a canoe to fetch him back," he said. "That is Bucongo's territory, and I don't trust the devil."

"Which one – Bones or Bucongo?" asked Hamilton innocently.

But Sanders was not feeling humorous.

At that precise moment Bones was sitting before the most fantastic religious assembly that ecclesiastic or layman had ever attended.

Fate and Bones had led the girl through a very pleasant forest glade – they left the light-draught *Wiggle* half a mile down stream owing to the shoals which barred their progress, and had come upon Bucongo in an exalted moment.

With the assurance that he was doing no more than intrude upon one of those meetings which the missionizing Chief of the Lesser Isisi so frequently held, Bones stood on the outer fringe of the circle which sat in silence to watch an unwilling novitiate getting acquainted with Bucongo's god.

The novice was a girl, and she lay before an altar of stones surmounted by a misshapen *beti* who glared with his one eye upon the devout gathering. The novice lay rigid, for the excellent reason that she was roped foot and hands to two pegs in the ground.

Before the altar itself was a fire of wood in which two irons were heating.

Bones did not take this in for a moment, for he was gazing open-mouthed at Bucongo. On his head was an indubitable mitre, but around the mitre was bound a strip of skin from which was suspended a circle of dangling monkey tails. For cope he wore a leopard's robe. His face was streaked red with camwood, and around his eyes he had painted two white circles.

He was in the midst of a frenzied address when the two white visitors came upon the scene, and his hand was outstretched to take the red branding-iron when the girl at Bones' side, with a little gasp of horror, broke into the circle, and wrenching the rough iron from the attendant's hand, flung it towards the circle of spectators, which widened in consequence.

"How dare you – how dare you!" she demanded breathlessly, "you horrible-looking man!"

Bucongo glared at her but said nothing; then he turned to meet Bones.

In that second of time Bucongo had to make a great decision, and to overcome the habits of a lifetime. Training and education to the dominion of the white man half raised his hand to the salute; something that boiled and bubbled madly and set his shallow brain afire, something that was of his ancestry, wild, unreasoning, brutish, urged other action. Bones had his revolver half drawn when the knobbly end of the chief's killing-spear struck him between the eyes, and he went down on his knees.

Thus it came about, that he found himself sitting before Bucongo, his hands and feet tied with native grass, with the girl at his side in no better case.

She was very frightened, but this she did not show. She had the disadvantage of being unable to understand the light flow of offensive badinage which passed between her captor and Bones.

"O Tibbetti," said Bucongo, "you see me as a god – I have finished with all white men."

"Soon we shall finish with you, Bucongo," said Bones.

"I cannot die, Tibbetti," said the other with easy confidence, "that is the wonderful thing."

"Other men have said that," said Bones in the vernacular, "and their widows are wives again and have forgotten their widowhood."

"This is a new ju-ju, Tibbetti," said Bucongo, a strange light in his eyes. "I am the greatest of all cross-God men, and it is revealed to me that many shall follow me. Now you and the woman shall be the first of all white people to bear the mark of Bucongo the Blessed. And in the days to be you shall bear your breasts and say, 'Bucongo the Wonderful did this with his beautiful hands.'"

Bones was in a cold sweat and his mouth was dry. He scarcely dare look at the girl by his side.

"What does he say?" she asked in a low voice. Bones hesitated, and then haltingly he stammered the translation of the threat.

She nodded.

"O Bucongo," said Bones, with a sudden inspiration, "though you do evil, I will endure. But this you shall do and serve me. Brand me alone upon the chest, and upon the back. For if we be branded separately we are bound to one another, and you see how ugly this woman is with her thin nose and her pale eyes; also she has long hair like the grass which the weaver birds use for their nests."

He spoke loudly, eagerly, and it seemed convincingly, for Bucongo was in doubt. Truly the woman by all standards was very ugly. Her face was white and her lips thin. She was a narrow woman too, he thought, like one underfed.

"This you will do for me, Bucongo," urged Bones; "for gods do not do evil things, and it would be bad to marry me to this ugly woman who has no hips and has an evil tongue."

Bucongo was undecided.

"A god may do no evil," he said; "but I do not know the ways of white men. If it be true, then I shall mark you twice Tibbetti, and you shall be my man for ever; and the woman I will not touch."

"Cheer oh!"said Bones.

"What are you saying – will he let us go?" asked the girl.

"I was sayin' what a jolly row there'll be," lied Bones; "and he was sayin' that he couldn't think of hurtin' a charmin' lady like you. Shut your eyes, dear old Miss Hamilton."

She shut them quickly, half fainting with terror, for Bucongo was coming towards them, a blazing iron in his hand, a smile of simple benevolence upon his not unintelligent face.

"This shall come as a blessing to you, Tibbetti," he said almost jovially.

Bones shut his teeth and waited.

The hot iron was scorching his silk shirt when a voice hailed the high-priest of the newest of cults.

"O Bucongo," it said.

Bucongo turned with a grimace of fear and cringed backward before the levelled Colt of Mr Commissioner Sanders.

"Tell me now," said Sanders in his even tone, "can such a man as you die? Think, Bucongo."

"Lord," said Bucongo huskily, "I think I can die."

"We shall see," said Sanders.

It was not until after dinner that night that the girl had recovered sufficiently to discuss her exciting morning.

"I think you were an awful brute," she addressed her unabashed brother. "You were standing in the wood listening to and seeing everything, and never came till the last minute."

"It was my fault," interrupted Sanders. "I wanted to see how far the gentle Bucongo would go."

"Dooced thoughtless," murmured Bones under his breath, but audible.

She looked at him long and earnestly then turned again to her brother.

32

"There is one thing I want to know," she said. "What was Bones saying when he talked to that horrible man? Do you know that Bones was scowling at me as though I was...I hardly know how to express it. Was he saying nice things?"

Hamilton looked up at the awning, and cleared his throat.

"Play the game, dear old sir and brother-officer," croaked Bones.

"He said – " began Hamilton.

"Live and let live," pleaded Bones, all of a twitter. "*Esprit de corps* an' discretion, jolly old captain."

Hamilton looked at his subordinate steadily.

"He asked to be branded twice in order that you might not be branded once," he said quietly.

The girl stared at Bones, and her eyes were full of tears.

"Oh, Bones!" she said, with a little catch in her voice, "you...you are a sportsman."

"Carry on," said Bones incoherently, and wept a little at the realization of that magnificent moment.

# THE MAKER OF STORMS

Everybody knows that water drawn from rivers is very bad water, for the rivers are the Roads of the Dead, and in the middle of those nights when the merest rind of a moon shows, and this slither of light and two watchful stars form a triangle pointing to the earth, the spirits rise from their graves and walk, "singing deadly songs," towards the lower star which is the source of all rivers. If you should be – which God forbid – on one of these lonely island graveyards on such nights you will see strange sights.

The broken cooking pots which rest on the mounds and the rent linen which flutters from little sticks stuck about the graves, grow whole and new again. The pots are red and hot as they come from the fire, and the pitiful cloths take on the sheen of youth and fold themselves about invisible forms. None may see the dead, though it is said that you may see the babies.

These the wise men have watched playing at the water's edge, crowing and chuckling in the universal language of their kind, staggering groggily along the shelving beach with outspread arms balancing their uncertain steps. On such nights when M'sa beckons the dead world to the source of all rivers, the middle islands are crowded with babies – the dead babies of a thousand years. Their spirits come up from the unfathomed deeps of the great river and call their mortality from the graves.

"How may the waters of the river be acceptable?" asks the shuddering N'gombi mother.

Therefore the N'gombi gather their water from the skies in strange cisterns of wicker, lined with the leaf of a certain plant which is impervious, and even carry their drinking supplies with them when they visit the river itself.

There was a certain month in the year, which will be remembered by all who attempted the crossing of the Kasai Forest to the south of the N'gombi country, when pools and rivulets suddenly dried – so suddenly, indeed, that even the crocodiles, who have an instinct for coming drought, were left high and dry, in some cases miles from the nearest water, and when the sun rose in a sky unflecked by cloud and gave place at nights to a sky so brilliant and so menacing in their fierce and fiery nearness that men went mad.

Toward the end of this month, when an exasperating full moon advertised a continuance of the dry spell by its very whiteness, the Chief Koosoogolaba-Muchini, or, as he was called, Muchini, summoned a council of his elder men, and they came with parched throats and fear of death.

"All men know," said Muchini, "what sorrow has come to us, for there is a more powerful ju-ju in the land than I remember. He has made M'shimba M'Shamba afraid so that he has gone away and walks no more in the forest with his terrible lightning. Also K'li, the father of pools, has gone into the earth and all his little children, and I think we shall die, every one of us."

There was a skinny old man, with a frame like a dried goatskin, who made a shuffling noise when he spoke.

"O Muchini," he said, "when I was a young man there was a way to bring M'shimba M'shamba which was most wonderful. In those days we took a young maiden and hung her upon a tree – "

"Those old ways were good," interrupted Muchini; "but I tell you M'bonia, that we can follow no more the old ways since Sandi came to the land, for he is a cruel man and hanged my own mother's brother for that fine way of yours. Yet we cannot sit and die because of certain magic which the Stone Breaker is practising."

Now Bula Matadi ("The Stone Breaker") was in those days the mortal enemy of the N'gombi people, who were wont to ascribe all their misfortunes to his machinations. To Bula Mutadi (which was the generic name by which the Government of the Congo Free State was known) was traceable the malign perversity of game, the blight of crops, the depredations of weaver birds. Bula Matadi encouraged leopards to attack isolated travellers, and would on great occasions change the seasons of the year that the N'gombi's gardens might come to ruin.

"It is known from one end of the earth to the other that I am a most cunning man," Muchini went on, stroking his muscular arm, a trick of self-satisfied men in their moments of complacence; "and whilst even the old men slept, I, Koosoogolaba-Muchini, the son of the terrible and crafty G'sombo, the brother of Eleni-N'gombi, I went abroad with my wise men and my spies and sought out devils and ghosts in places where even the bravest have never been," he lowered his voice to a horse whisper, "to the Ewa-Ewa Mongo, the Very Place of Death."

The gasp of horror from his audience was very satisfying to this little chief of the Inner N'gombi, and here was a moment suitable for his climax.

"And behold!" he cried.

By his side was something covered with a piece of native cloth. This covering he removed with a flourish and revealed a small yellow box.

It was most certainly no native manufacture, for its angles were clamped with neat brass corner-pieces set flush in the polished wood.

The squatting councillors watched their lord as with easy familiarity he opened the lid.

There were twenty tiny compartments, and in each was a slender glass tube, corked and heavily sealed, whilst about the neck of each tube was a small white label covered with certain devil marks.

Muchini waited until the sensation he had prepared had had its full effect.

"By the Great River which runs to the Allamdani,"* he said slowly and impressively, "were white men who had been sent by Bula Matadi to catch ghosts. For I saw them, I and my wise men, when the moon

---

* This was evidently the Sanga River

36

was calling all spirits. They were gathered by the river with little nets and little gourds and they caught the waters. Also they caught little flies and other foolish things and took them to their tent. Then my young men and I waited, and when all were gone away we went to their tents and found this magic box – which is full of devils and great power – Ro!"

He leapt to his feet, his eye gleaming. Across the starry dome of the sky there had flicked a quick flare of light.

There came a sudden uneasy stirring of leaves, a hushed whisper of things as though the forest had been suddenly awakened from sleep.

Then an icy cold breeze smote his cheek, and staring upward, he saw the western stars disappearing in swathes behind the tumbling clouds.

"M'shimba M'shamba – he lives!" he roared, and the crash of thunder in the forest answered him.

Bosambo, Chief of the Ochori, was on the furthermost edge of the forest, for he was following the impulse of his simple nature and was hunting in a country where he had no right to be. The storm (which he cursed, having no scruples about river and water, and being wholly sceptical as to ghosts) broke with all its fury over his camp and passed. Two nights later, he sat before the rough hut his men had built, discussing the strange ways of the antelope, when he suddenly stopped and listened, lowering his head till it almost touched the ground.

Clear to his keen ears came the rattle of the distant lokali – the drum that sends messages from village to village and from nation to nation.

"O Secundi," said Bosambo, with a note of seriousness in his voice, "I have not heard that call for many moons – for it is the war call of the N'gombi."

"Lord, it is no war call," said the old man, shifting his feet for greater comfort, "yet it is a call which may mean war, for it calls spears to a dance, and it is strange, for the N'gombi have no enemies."

"All men are the enemies of the N'gombi," Bosambo quoted a river saying as old as the sun.

He listened again, and rose.

"You shall go back and gather me a village of spears, and bring them to the borderland near the road that crosses the river," he said.

"On my life," said the other.

Muchini, Chief of the Inner N'gombi, a most inflated man and a familiar of magical spirits, gathered his spears to some purpose, for two days later Bosambo met him by his border and the chiefs greeted one another between two small armies.

"Which way do you go, Muchini?" asked Bosambo.

Now, between Muchini and the Chief of the Ochori was a grievance dating back to the big war, when Bosambo had slain the N'gombi chief of the time with his own hands.

"I go to the river to call a palaver of all free men," said Muchini; "for I tell you this, Bosambo, that I have found a great magic which will make us greater than Sandi, and it has been prophesied that I shall be king over a thousand times a thousand spears. For I have a small box which brings even M'shimba to my call."

Bosambo, a head and shoulders taller than the other, waved his hand towards the forest path which leads eventually to the Ochori city.

"Here is a fine moment for you, Muchini," he said, "and you shall try your great magic on me and upon my young men. For I say that you do not go by this way, neither you nor your warriors, since I am the servant of Sandi and of his King, and he has sent me here to keep his peace; go back to your village, for this is the way to Death."

Muchini glared at his enemy.

"Yet this way I go, Bosambo," he said huskily, and looked over his shoulder towards his followers.

Bosambo swung round on one heel, an arm and a leg outstretched in the attitude of an athlete who is putting the shot. Muchini threw up his wicker shield and pulled back his stabbing spear, but he was a dead man before the weapon was poised.

Thus ended the war, and the N'gombi folk went home, never so much as striking a blow for the yellow box which Bosambo claimed for himself as his own personal loot.

At the time, Mr Commissioner Sanders, CMG, was blissfully ignorant of the miraculous happenings which have been recorded. He was wholly preoccupied by the novelty which the presence of Patricia Hamilton offered. Never before had a white woman made her home at the Residency, and it changed things a little.

She was at times an embarrassment.

When Fubini, the witch-doctor of the Akasava, despatched five maidens to change Sandi's wicked heart – Sanders had sent Fubini to the Village of Irons for six months for preaching unauthorized magic – they came, in the language of Bones, "doocedly undressed," and Patricia had beaten a hurried retreat.

She was sometimes an anxiety, as I have already shown, but was never a nuisance. She brought to headquarters an aroma of English spring, a clean fragrance that refreshed the heat-jaded Commissioner and her brother, but which had no perceptible influence upon Bones.

That young officer called for her one hot morning, and Hamilton, sprawling on a big cane chair drawn to the shadiest and breeziest end of the verandah, observed that Bones carried a wooden box, a drawing-board, a pad of paper, two pencils imperfectly concealed behind his large ear, and a water-bottle.

"Shop!" said Hamilton lazily. "Forward, Mr Bones – what can we do for you this morning?"

Bones shaded his eyes and peered into the cool corner. "Talkin' in your sleep, dear old Commander," he said pleasantly, "dreamin' of the dear old days beyond recall."

He struck an attitude and lifted his unmusical voice –

> "When life was gay, heigho!
> Tum tum te tay, heigho!
> Oh, tiddly umpty humpty umpty do,
> When life was gay – dear old officer – heigho!"

Patricia Hamilton stepped out to the verandah in alarm. "Oh, please, don't make that hooting noise," she appealed to her brother. "I'm writing –"

"Don't be afraid," said Hamilton, "it was only Bones singing. Do it again, Bones, Pat didn't hear you."

Bones stood erect, his hand to his white helmet.

"Come aboard, my lady," he said.

"I won't keep you a minute, Bones," said the girl, and disappeared into the house.

"What are you doing this morning?" asked Hamilton, gazing with pardonable curiosity at the box and drawing-board.

"Polishin' up my military studies with Miss Hamilton's kind assistance – botany and applied science, sir," said Bones briskly. "Field fortifications, judgin' distance, strategy, Bornongo grammar, field cookery an' tropical medicines."

"What has poor little making-up-company-accounts done?" asked Hamilton, and Bones blushed.

"Dear old officer," he begged, "I'll tackle that little job as soon as I get back. I tried to do 'em this mornin' an' was four dollars out – it's the regimental cash account that's wrong. People come in and out helpin' themselves, and I positively can't keep track of the money."

"As I'm the only person with the key of the regimental cash-box, I suppose you mean – ?"

Bones raised his hand.

"I make no accusations, dear old feller – it's a painful subject. We all have those jolly old moments of temptation. I tackle the accounts tonight, sir. You musn't forget that I've a temperament. I'm not like you dear old woodenheads – "

"Oh, shut up," said the weary Hamilton. "So long as you're going to do a bit of study, it's all right."

"Now, Bones," said Patricia, appearing on the scene, "have you got the sandwiches?"

Bones made terrifying and warning grimaces.

"Have you got the board to lay the cloth and the paper to cover it, and the chocolates and the cold tea?"

Bones frowned, and jerked his head in an agony of warning.

"Come on, then," said the unconscious betrayer of Lieutenant Tibbetts. "Goodbye, dear."

"Why 'goodbye,' dear old Hamilton's sister?" asked Bones.

She looked at him scornfully and led the way.

"Don't forget the field fortifications," called Hamilton after him; "they eat nicely between slices of strategy."

The sun was casting long shadows eastward when they returned. They had not far to come, for the place they had chosen for their picnic was well within the Residency reservation, but Bones had been describing on his way back one of the remarkable powers he possessed, namely, his ability to drag the truth from reluctant and culpable natives. And every time he desired to emphasize the point he would stop, lower all his impedimenta to the ground, cluttering up the landscape with picnic-box, drawing-board, sketching-blocks and the numerous bunches of wild flowers he had culled at her request, and press his argument with much palm-punching.

He stopped for the last time on the very edge of the barrack square, put down his cargo and proceeded to demolish the doubt she had unwarily expressed.

"That's where you've got an altogether erroneous view of me, dear old sister," he said triumphantly. "I'm known up and down the river as the one man that you can't deceive. Go up and ask the Bomongo, drop in on the Isisi, speak to the Akasava, an' what will they say? They'll say, 'No, ma'am, there's no flies on jolly old Bones − not on your life, Harriet!' "

"Then they would be very impertinent," smiled Pat.

"Ask Sanders (God bless him!). Ask Ham. Ask − " he was going on enthusiastically.

"Are you going to camp here, or are you coming in?" she challenged.

Bones gathered up his belongings, never ceasing to talk.

"Fellers like me, dear young friend, make the Empire − paint the whole bally thing red, white and blue − 'unhonoured and unsung, until the curtain's rung, the boys that made the Empire and the Navy.' "

"Bones, you promised you wouldn't sing," she said reproachfully; "and, besides, you're not in the navy."

"That doesn't affect the argument," protested Bones, and was rapidly shedding his equipment in preparation for another discourse, when she walked on towards Sanders who had come across the square to meet them.

Bones made a dive at the articles he had dropped, and came prancing (no other word describes his erratic run) up to Sanders.

"I've just been telling Miss Hamilton, sir and Excellency, that nobody can find things that old Bones – you'll remember, sir the episode of your lost pyjama legs. Who found 'em?"

"You did," said Sanders; "they were sent home in your washing. Talking about finding things, read this."

He handed a telegraph form to the young man, and Bones, peering into the message until his nose almost touched the paper, read –

Very urgent. Clear the line. Administration.
To Sanders, Commission River Territories. Message begins. Belgian Congo Government reports from Leopoldville, Bacteriological Expedition carriers raided on edge of your territory by Inner N'gombi people, all stores looted including case of 20 culture tubes. Stop. As all these cultures are of virulent diseases, inoculate Inner N'gombi until intact tubes recovered. Message ends.

Bones read it twice, and his face took on an appearance which indicated something between great pain and intense vacancy. It was intended to convey to the observer the fact that Bones was thinking deeply and rapidly, and that he had banished from his mind all the frivolities of life.

"I understand, sir – you wish me to go to the dear old Congo Government and apologize – I shall be ready in ten minutes."

"What I really want you to do," said Sanders patiently, "is to take the *Wiggle* up stream and get that box."

"I quite understand, sir," said Bones, nodding his head. "Today is the 8th, tomorrow is the 9th – the box shall be in your hands on the 15th by half-past seven in the evening, dear old sir."

He saluted and turned a baleful glare upon the girl, the import of which she was to learn at first hand.

"Duty, Miss Patricia Hamilton! Forgive poor old Bones if he suddenly drops the mask of *dolce far niente* – I go!"

He saluted again and went marching stiffly to his quarters, with all the dignity which an empty lunch-box and a dangling water-bottle would allow him.

The next morning Bones went forth importantly for the Ochori city, being entrusted with the task of holding, so to speak, the right flank of the N'gombi country.

"You will use your discretion," Sanders said at parting, "and, of course, you must keep your eyes open; if you hear the merest hint that the box is in your neighbourhood, get it."

"I think, your Excellency," said Bones, with heavy carelessness, "that I have fulfilled missions quite as delicate as this, and as for observation, why, the gift runs in my family."

"And runs so fast that you've never caught up with it," growled Hamilton.

Bones turned haughtily and saluted. It was a salute full of subdued offence.

He went joyously to the northward, evolving cunning plans. He stopped at every village to make inquiries and to put the unoffending villagers to considerable trouble – for he insisted upon a house-to-house search – before, somewhat wearied by his own zeal, he came to the Ochori.

Chief Bosambo heard of his coming and summoned his councillors.

"Truly has Sandi a hundred ears," he said in dismay, "for it seems that he has heard of the slaying of Muchini. Now, all men who are true to me will swear to the lord Tibbetti that we know nothing of a killing palaver, and that we have not been beyond the trees to the land side of the city. This you will say because you love me; and if any man says another thing I will beat him until he is sick."

Bones came and was greeted by the chief – and Bosambo was carried to the beach on a litter.

43

"Lord," said Bosambo weakly, "now the sight of your simple face will make me a well man again. For, lord, I have not left my bed since the coming of the rains, and there is strength neither in my hands and feet."

"Poor old bird," said Bones sympathetically, "you've been sittin' in a draught."

"This I tell you, Tibbetti," Bosambo went on, as yet uncertain of his ruler's attitude, since Bones must need, at this critical moment, employ English and idiomatic English, "that since the last moon was young I have lain in my hut never moving, seeing nothing and hearing nothing, being like a dead man – all this my headman will testify."

Bones' face dropped, for he had hoped to secure information here. Bosambo, watching his face through half-closed lids, saw the dismal droop of the other's mouth, and came to the conclusion that whatever might be the cause of the visit, it was not to hold the Ochori or their chief to account for known misdeeds.

"O Bosambo," said Bones, in the river dialect, "this is sad news, for I desire that you shall tell me certain things for which Sandi would have given you salt and rods."

The Chief of the Ochori sat up in his litter and went so far as to put one foot to the ground.

"Lord," he said heartily, "the sound of your lovely voice brings me from the grave and gives me strength. Ask, O Bonesi, for you are my father and my mother; and though I saw and heard nothing, yet in my sickness I had wonderful visions and all things were made visible – that I declare to you, Bonesi, before all men."

"Don't call me 'Bonesi,' " said Bones fiercely. "You're a jolly cheeky feller, Bosambo – you're very, very naughty, indeed!"

"Master," said Bosambo humbly, "though I rule these Ochori I am a foreigner in this land; in the tongue of my own people, Bonesi means 'he-who-is-noble-in-face-and-a-giver-of-justice'."

"That's better," nodded the gratified Bones, and went on speaking in the dialect. "You shall help me in this – it touches on the people of the Inner N'gombi – "

Bosambo fell back wearily on to the litter, and rolled his eyes as one in pain.

"This is a sorrow for me, Bo – Tibbetti," he said faintly, "but I am a sick man."

"Also," continued Bones, "of a certain box of wood, full of poisons – "

As well as he could Bones explained the peculiar properties of germ culture.

"Oh, ko!" said Bosambo, closing his eyes, and was to all appearances beyond human aid.

"Lord," said Bosambo, at parting, "you have brought me to life, and every man of every tribe shall know that you are a great healer. To all the far and quiet places of the forest I will send my young men who will cry you aloud as a most wonderful doctor."

"Not at all," murmured Bones modestly, "not at all."

"Master," said Bosambo, this time in English, for he was not to be outdone in the matter of languages, for had he not attended a great mission school in Monrovia? "Master, you dam' fine feller, you look 'um better feller, you no find um. You be same like Moses and Judi Escariot, big fine feller, by golly – yas."

All night long, between the visits which Bones had been making from the moored *Wiggle* to the village (feeling the patient's pulse with a profound and professional air and prescribing brandy and milk), Bosambo had been busy.

"Stand you at the door, Secundi," he said to his headman, "and let one of your men go to the shore to warn me of my lord Tibbetti's coming, for I have work to do. It seems this Maker of Storms were better with Sandi than with me."

"Tibbetti is a fool, I think," suggested Secundi.

Bosambo, kneeling on a rush mat, busy with a native chisel and a pot of clay paint, looked up.

"I have beaten older men than you with a stick until they have wept," he said, "and all for less than you say. For this is the truth, Secundi, that a child cannot be a fool, though an old man may be a shame. This is the word of the blessed prophet. As for Tibbetti, he has a clean and loving heart."

There was a rustle at the door and a whispered voice. The box and the tools were thrust under a skin rug and Bosambo again became the interesting invalid.

In the morning Bosambo had said farewell, and a blushing Bones listened with unconcealed pleasure to the extravagant praise of his patient.

"And this I tell you, Tibbetti," said Bosambo, standing thigh-deep in the river by the launch's side, "that knowing you are wise man who gathers wisdom, I have sent to the end of my country for some rare and beautiful thing that you may carry it with you."

He signalled to a man on the bank, and his servant brought him a curious object.

It was, Bones noted, a square box apparently of native make, for it was fantastically carved and painted. There were crude heads and hideous forms which were never on land or sea. The paint was brilliant; red, yellow and green indiscriminately splashed.

"This is very ancient and was brought to my country by certain forest people. It is a Maker of Storms, and is a powerful ju-ju for good and evil."

Bones, already a collector of native work, was delighted. His delight soothed him for his failure in other respects.

He returned to headquarters empty-handed and sat the centre of a chilling group – if we except Patricia Hamilton – and endeavoured, as so many successful advocates have done, to hide his shortcomings behind a screen of rhetoric.

He came to the part in his narrative where Bosambo was taken ill without creating any notable sensation, save that Sanders' grey eyes narrowed a little and he paid greater heed to the rest of the story.

"There was poor old Bosambo knocked out, sir – ab-so-lutely done for – fortunately I did not lose my nerve. You know what I am, dear old officer, in moments of crisis?"

"I know," said Hamilton grimly, "something between a Welsh revivalist and a dancing dervish."

"Please go on, Bones," begged the girl, not the least interested of the audience.

"I dashed straight back to the *Wiggle*," said Bones breathlessly, "searched for my medicine chest – it wasn't there! Not so much as a mustard plaster – what was I to do, dear old Miss Hamilton?" he appealed dramatically.

"Don't tell him, Pat," begged Hamilton, "he's sure to guess it."

"What was I to do? I seized a bottle of brandy," said Bones with relish, "I dashed back to where Bosambo was lyin', I dashed into the village, into his hut and got a glass – "

"Well, well!" said Sanders impatiently, "what happened after all this dashing?"

Bones spread out his hands.

"Bosambo is alive today," he said simply, "praisin' – if I may be allowed to boast – the name of Bones the Medicine Man. Look here, sir."

He dragged towards him along the floor of the hut a package covered with a piece of native sacking. This he whisked away and revealed the hideous handiwork of an artist who had carved and painted as true to nature as a man may who is not quite certain whether the human eye is half-way down the nose or merely an appendage to his ear.

"That, sir," said Bones impressively, "is one of the most interestin' specimens of native work I have ever seen: a gift! From Bosambo to the jolly old doctor man who dragged him, if I might so express it, from the very maws of death."

He made his dramatic pause.

Sanders bent down, took a penknife from his pocket and scraped the paint from a flat oblong space on the top.

There for all men to see – save Bones who was now engaged in a relation of his further adventure to his one sympathizer – was a brass plate, and when the paint had been scraped away, an inscription – *Department du Médicins, Etat CONGO BELGE.*

Sanders and Hamilton gazed, fascinated and paralysed to silence.

"I've always had a feelin' I'd like to be a medicine man," Bones prattled on. "You see – "

"One moment, Bones," interrupted Sanders quietly. "Did you open this box by any chance?"

"No, sir," said Bones.

"And did you see any of its contents?"

"No, sir," said Bones confidentially, "that's the most interestin' thing about the box. It contains magic – which, of course, honoured sir and Excellency, is all rubbish."

Sanders took a bunch of keys from his pocket, and after a few trials opened the case and scrutinized the contents, noting the comforting fact that all the tubes were sealed. He heaved a deep sigh of thankfulness.

"You didn't by chance discover anything about the missing cultures, Bones?" he asked mildly.

Bones shook his head, shrugged his shoulders, and looked disconsolately at his chief.

"You think I've been feeble, but I haven't lost hope, sir," he said, with fine resolution. "I've got a feelin' that if I were allowed to go into the forest, disguised, sir, as a sort of half-witted native chap, sir – "

"Disguised!" said Hamilton, "Good Lord, what do you want a disguise for?"

# BONES AND THE WIRELESS

Ko-boru, the headman of Bingini, called his relations together for a solemn family conference.

The lower river folk play an inconsiderable role in the politics of the Territories, partly because they are so near to headquarters that there is no opportunity for any of those secret preparations which precede all native intrigues, great or small, and partly because the lower river people are so far removed from the turbulent elements of the upper river that they are not swayed by the cyclonic emotions of the Isisi, the cold and deliberate desire for slaughter which is characteristically Akasavian, or the electrical decisions of the Outer N'gombi.

But they had their crises.

To Bingini came all the notables of the district who claimed kinship with Ko-buru, and they sat in a great circle about the headman's hut, alternately eyeing the old headman and their stout relative, his daughter.

"All my relations shall know this," began Koboru, after Okmimi, the witch-doctor, had formally burnt away the devils and ghosts that fringe all large assemblies, "that a great shame has come to us, every one, because of Yoka-m'furi. For this Yoka is to Sandi as a brother, and guides his little ship up and down the river, and because of this splendid position I gave him my own daughter by the first of my wives."

"S'm-m!" murmured the council in agreement.

49

"Also I built him a hut and gave him a garden, where his wife might work, and he has sat at family palavers. Now, I tell you that Yoka-m'furi is an evil man, for he has left my daughter, and has found another wife in the upper river, and he comes no more to this village, and my daughter weeps all day.

"For three seasons he has not been to this village; when the moon comes again, it will be four." He said this with proper significance, and the flat face of the melancholy girl by his side puckered and creased miserably before she opened her large mouth to wail her woe.

For the man who deliberately separates himself from his wife for four seasons and does not spend twenty-four hours – "from sunrise to moonset" in her village is automatically divorced and freed from all responsibility. This is the custom of all people from the lands of the Great King to the sea.

"Now, I have had a dream," Ko-boru went on, "and in this dream it was told me that I should call you all together, and that I and the chief of my councillors and friends should go to Sandi and tell him what is true."

"Brother and uncle," said Bechimi of G'lara, "I will go with you, for once I spoke to Sandi and he spoke to me, and because of his cunning memory he will recall Bechimi, who picked up his little black stick, when it fell, and gave it to him."

Five were chosen to accompany Ko-boru, and they took canoe and travelled for less than five miles to the Residency.

Sanders was entertaining Patricia Hamilton with stories of native feuds, when the unexpected deputation squatted in the sun before the verandah.

"O Ko-boru," hailed Sanders, "why do you come?"

Ko-boru was all for a long and impressive palaver, but recognized a certain absence of encouragement in the Commissioner's tone. Therefore he came straight to the point.

"Now, you are our father and our mother, Sandi," he said, in conclusion, "and when you speak, all wonders happen. Also you have very beautiful friends, Militini, who speak a word and set his terrible soldiers moving like leopards towards a kill, and Tibbetti, the young one who is innocent and simple. So I say to you, Sandi, that if you speak one word to Yoka, he will come back to my daughter, his wife."

Sanders stood by the rail of the stoep and looked down upon the spokesman.

"I hear strange things, Ko-boru," he said quietly. "They tell me stories of a woman with many lovers and an evil tongue; and once there came to me Yoka with a wounded head, for this daughter of yours is very quick in her anger."

"Lord," said the flustered Ko-boru, "such things happen even in love."

"All things happen in love," said Sanders, with a little smile, "and, if it is to be, Yoka will return. Also, if it is to be, he will not go back to the woman, and she will be free. This palaver is finished."

"Lord," pleaded Ko-buru, "the woman will do no more angry things. Let him come back from sunrise to moonset – "

"This palaver is finished," repeated Sanders.

On the way back to Bingini the relatives of Ko-boru made a plot. It was the first plot that had been hatched in the shadow of headquarters for twenty years.

"Would it be indiscreet to ask what your visitors wanted?" asked the girl, as the crestfallen deputation was crossing the square to their canoe.

"It was a marriage palaver," replied Sanders, with a little grimace, "and I was being requested to restore a husband to a temperamental lady who has a passion for shying cook-pots at her husband when she is annoyed."

The girl's laughing eyes were fixed upon his.

"Poor Mr Sanders!" she said, with mock seriousness.

"Don't be sorry for me," smiled Sanders. "I'm rather domestic really, and I'm interested in this case because the man concerned is my steersman – the best on the river, and a capital all-round man. Besides that," he went on seriously, "I regard them all as children of mine. It is right that a man who shirks his individual responsibilities to the race should find a family to 'father.' "

"Why do you?" she asked, after a little pause.

"Why do I what?"

"Shirk your responsibilities," she said. "This is a healthy and delightful spot: a woman might be very happy here."

There was an awkward silence.

"I'm afraid I've been awfully impertinent," said Patricia, hurriedly rising, "but to a woman there is a note of interrogation behind every bachelor – especially nice bachelors – and the more 'confirmed' he is, the bigger the question mark."

Sanders rose to her.

"One of these days I shall do something rash," he threatened with that shy laugh of his. "Here is *your* little family coming."

Bones and Hamilton were discussing something heatedly, and justice was on the side of Lieutenant Tibbetts, if one could judge by the frequency with which he stopped and gesticulated.

"It really is too bad," said the annoyed Hamilton, as he mounted the steps to the stoep, followed by Bones, who, to do him justice, did not adopt the attitude of a delinquent, but was, on the contrary, injured virtue personified.

"What is too bad, dear?" asked the girl sympathetically.

"A fortnight ago," said Hamilton, "I told this sillyass – "

"Your jolly old brother is referrin' to me, dear lady," explained Bones.

"Who else could I be referring to?" demanded the other truculently. "I told him to have all the company accounts ready by tomorrow. You know, sir, that the paymaster is coming down from Administration to check 'em, and will you believe me, sir" – he glared at Bones, who immediately closed his eyes resignedly – "would you believe me that, when I went to examine those infernal accounts, they were all at sixes and sevens?"

"Threes an' nines, dear old officer," murmured Bones, waking up, "the matter in dispute being a trifle of thirty-nine dollars, which I have generously offered to make up out of my own pocket."

He beamed round as one who expected applause.

"And on top of this," fumed Hamilton, "he talks of taking Pat for an early morning picnic to the village island!"

"Accompanied by the jolly old accounts," corrected Bones. "Do me justice, sir and brother-officer. I offered to take the books with me, an' render a lucid and convincin' account of my stewardship."

"Don't make me laugh," snarled Hamilton, stamping into the bungalow.

"Isn't he naughty?" said Bones admiringly.

"Now, Bones," warned the girl, "I shan't go unless you keep your word with Alec."

Bones drew himself up and saluted.

"Dear old friend," he said proudly, "put your faith in Bones."

"HM Launch No. 36 (Territories)," as it was officially described on the stores record, had another name, which she earned in her early days through certain eccentricities of construction. Though she might not in justice be called the *Wiggle* any longer, yet the *Wiggle* she was from one end of the river to the other, and even native men called her "Komfuru," which means "that which does not run straight."

It had come to be recognized that the *Wiggle* was the especial charge of Lieutenant Tibbetts. Bones himself was the first to recognize this right. There were moments when he inferred that the *Wiggle's* arrival on the station at the time he was making his own first appearance was something more than a coincidence.

She was not, in the strictest sense of the word, a launch, for she possessed a square, open dining-saloon and two tiny cabins amidships. Her internal works were open to the light of day, and her engineer lived in the engine-room up to his waist and on deck from his waist up, thus demonstrating the possibility of being in two places at once.

The *Wiggle*, moreover, possessed many attributes which are denied to other small steamers. She had, for example, a Maxim gun on her tiny forecastle. She had a siren of unusual power and diabolical tone, she was also fitted with a big motor-horn, both of which appendages were Bones' gift to his flagship. The motor-horn may seem superfluous, but when the matter is properly explained, you will understand the necessity for some less drastic method of self-advertisement than the siren.

The first time the siren had been fitted Bones had taken the *Wiggle* through "the Channel." Here the river narrows and deepens, and the current runs at anything from five to seven knots an hour. Bones was going up stream, and met the Bolalo Mission steamer coming down. She had dipped her flag to the *Wiggle's* blue ensign, and Bones had replied with two terrific blasts on his siren.

After that the *Wiggle* went backwards, floating with the current all ways, from broadside on to stern first, for in those two blasts Bones had exhausted the whole of his steam reserve.

She was also equipped with wireless. There was an "aerial" and an apparatus which Bones had imported from England at a cost of twelve pounds, and which was warranted to receive messages from two hundred miles distant. There was also a book of instructions. Bones went to his hut with the book and read it. His servant found him in bed the next morning, sleeping like a child, with his hand resting lightly upon the second page.

Sanders and Hamilton both took a hand at fixing the *Wiggle's* wireless. The only thing they were all quite certain about was that there ought to be a wire somewhere. So they stretched the aerial from the funnel to the flagstaff at the stern of the boat, and then addressed themselves to the less simple solution of "making it work."

They tried it for a week, and gave it up in despair.

"They've had you, Bones," said Hamilton. "It doesn't 'went.' Poor old Bones!"

"Your pity, dear old officer, is offensive," said Bones stiffly, "an' I don't mind tellin' you that I've a queer feelin' – I can't explain what it is, except that I'm a dooce of a psychic – that that machine is goin' to be jolly useful."

But though Bones worked day and night, read the book of instructions from cover to cover, and took the whole apparatus to pieces, examining each part under a strong magnifying glass, he never succeeded either in transmitting or receiving a message, and the machine was repacked and stored in the spare cabin, and was never by any chance referred to, except by Hamilton in his most unpleasant moments.

Bones took an especial delight in the *Wiggle*; it was his very own ship, and he gave her his best personal attention.

It was Bones who ordered from London especially engraved notepaper headed "HMS *Komfuru*" – the native name sounded more important than *Wiggle*, and more important than "Launch 36." It was Bones who installed the little dynamo which – when it worked – lit the cabins and even supplied power for a miniature searchlight. It was Bones who had her painted Service grey, and would have added another funnel if Hamilton had not detected the attempted aggrandizement. Bones claimed that she was dustproof, waterproof, and torpedo-proof, and Hamilton had voiced his regret that she was not also fool-proof.

At five o'clock the next morning, when the world was all big hot stars and shadows, and there was no sound but the whisper of the running river and the "ha-a-a-a – ha-a-a-a" of breakers, Bones came from his hut, crossed the parade ground, and, making his way by the light of a lantern along the concrete quay – it was the width of an average table – dropped on to the deck and kicked the custodian of the *Wiggle* to wakefulness.

Bones' satellite was one Ali Abid, who was variously described as Moor, Egyptian, Tripolitan, and Bedouin, but was by all ethnological indications a half-breed Kano, who had spent the greater part of his life in the service of a professor of bacteriology. This professor was something of a purist, and the association with Ali Abid, plus a grounding in the elementary subjects which are taught at St Joseph's Mission School, Cape Coast Castle, had given Ali a gravity of demeanour and a splendour of vocabulary which many better favoured than he might have envied.

"Arise," quoth Bones, in the cracked bass which he employed whenever he felt called upon to deliver his inaccurate versions of Oriental poets –

> *"Arise, for morning in the bowl of night*
> *Has chucked a stone to put the stars to flight.*
> *And lo! and lo!…Get up, Ali the caravan is moving.*
> *Oh make haste!"*

("Omar will never be dead so long as Bones quotes him," Hamilton once said; "he simply couldn't afford to be dead and leave it to Bones!")

Ali rose, blinking and shivering, for the early morning was very cold, and he had been sleeping under an old padded dressing-gown which Bones had donated.

"Muster all the hands," said Bones, setting his lantern on the deck.

"Sir," said Ali slowly, "the subjects are not at our disposition. Your preliminary instructions presupposed that you had made necessary arrangements *re personnel.*"

Bones scratched his head.

"Dash my whiskers," he said in his annoyance, "didn't I tell you that I was taking the honourable lady for a trip? Didn't I tell you, you jolly old slacker, to have everything ready by daybreak? Didn't I issue explicit an' particular instructions about grub?"

"Sir," said Ali, "you didn't."

"Then," said Bones wrathfully, "why the dickens do I think I have?"

"Sir," said Ali, "some subjects, when enjoying refreshing coma, possess delirium, hallucinations, highly imaginative, which dissipate when the subject recovers consciousness, but retain in brain cavity illusory reminiscences."

Bones thrust his face into the others.'

"Do you mean to tell me I dreamt it?" he hissed.

"Sir," said Ali, "self-preservation compels complete acquiescence in your diagnosis."

"You're childish," said Bones.

He gave a few vague instructions in the best Bones manner, and stole up to the dark Residency. He had solemnly promised Sanders that he would rouse the girl without waking the rest of the house.

They were to go up stream to the Village Island, where the ironworkers of the Akasava had many curious implements to show her. Breakfast was to be taken on the boat, and they were to return for tiffin.

Overnight she had shown Bones the window of her room, and Hamilton had offered to make a chalk mark on the sash, so there could be no mistaking the situation of the room.

"If you wake me before sunrise, I shall do something I shall be sorry for," he warned Bones. "If you return without straightening the accounts, I shall do something which *you* will be sorry for."

Bones remembered this as he crept stealthily along the wooden verandah. To make doubly sure, he took off his boots and dropped them with a crash.

"Sh!" said Bones loudly. "Sh, Bones! Not so much noise, you silly old ass!"

He crept softly along the wooden wall and reconnoitred. The middle window was Hamilton's room, the left was Sanders', the right was Patricia's. He went carefully to the right window and knocked. There was no answer. He knocked again. Still no reply. He knocked loudly.

"Is that you, Bones?" growled Sanders' voice.

Bones gasped.

"Awfully sorry, sir," he whispered agitatedly – "my mistake entirely."

He tiptoed to the left window and rapped smartly. Then he whistled, then he rapped again.

He heard a bed creak, and turned his head modestly away. "It's Bones, dear old sister," he said, in his loudest whisper. "Arise, for mornin' in the bowl of light has – "

Hamilton's voice raged at him.

"I knew it was you, you blithering –"

"Dear old officer," began Bones, "awfully sorry! Go to sleep again. Night-night!"

"Go to the devil!" said a muffled voice.

Bones, however, went to the middle window; here he could make no mistake. He knocked authoritatively.

"Hurry up, ma'am," he said; "time is on the wing – "

The sash was flung up, and again Bones confronted the furious Hamilton.

"Sir," said the exasperated Bones, "how the dooce did you get here?"

"Don't you know this room has two windows? I told you last night, you goop! Pat sleeps at the other end of the building. I told you that, too, but you've got a brain like wool!"

"I am obliged to you, sir," said Bones, on his dignity, "for the information. I will not detain you."

Hamilton groped on his dressing-table for a hair-brush.

"Go back to bed, sir," said Bones, "an' don't forget to say your prayers."

He was searching for the window in the other wing of the Residency, when the girl, who had been up and dressed for a quarter of an hour, came softly behind him and tapped him on the shoulder.

"Wow!" screeched Bones. "Oh, Lord, dear old sister, you gave me the dickens of a fright! Well, let's get along. Thank heavens, we haven't disturbed anybody."

He was followed to the boat with the imprecations of two pyjamaed figures that stood on the stoep and watched his lank body melt in the darkness.

"Send us a wireless when you're coming back!" roared Hamilton.

"Cad!" said Bones, between his teeth.

Ali Abid had not been idle. He had aroused Yoka, the steersman, and Boosoobi, the engineer, and these two men had accepted the unexpected call with the curious readiness which natives show on such occasions, and which suggests that they have pre-knowledge of the summons, and are only waiting the word.

In one of the small cabins Ali had arranged the much discussed company accounts ready for his lord's attention, and there was every promise of a happy and a profitable day when Yoka rang the engines "ahead," and the *Wiggle* jerked her way to midstream.

The east had grown pale, there was a murmur from the dark forests on either bank, the timorous chirping or bad tempered squawk of a bird, a faint fragrance of burning gumwood from the fishing villages established on the river bank, where, in dancing spots of light, the women were tending to their fires.

There is no intermediate stage on the big river between darkness and broad daylight. The stars go out all at once, and the inky sky which serves then becomes a delicate blue. The shadows melt deeper and deeper into the forest, clearly revealing the outlines of the straight-stemmed trees. There is just this interregnum of pearl greyness, a sort of hush-light, which lasts whilst a man counts twenty, before the silver lances of the sun are flashing through the leaves, and the grey veil which blurs the islands to shapeless blotches in a river of dull silver is burnt to nothingness, and the islands are living things of vivid green set in waters of gold.

"The sunrise!" said Bones, and waved his hand to the east with the air of one who was responsible for the miracle.

The girl sat in a deep wicker chair and breathed in the glory and freshness of the scene. Across the broad river, right ahead of the boat, a flock of parroquets was flying, screeching their raucous chorus. The sun caught their brilliant plumage, and she saw, as it seemed, a rainbow in flight.

"Isn't that wonderful?" she whispered.

Bones peered up at the birds, shading his eyes.

"Just like a jolly old patchwork quilt," he said. "What a pity they can't talk till you teach 'em! They're awful bad eatin', too, though some fellers say they make a good curry – "

"Oh look, look!"

The *Wiggle* was swerving to the southern bank of the river, and two majestic flamingos standing at the water's edge had arrested the girl's attention.

"*They're* bad eatin', too," said the informative Bones. "The flesh is fishy an' too fat; heron are just the same."

"Haven't you a soul, Bones?" she asked severely.

59

"A soul, dear ma'am?" Bones asked, in astonishment. "Why, that's my speciality!"

It was a delightful morning for the girl, for Bones had retired to his cabin at her earnest request, and was struggling with the company accounts, and she was left to enjoy the splendour of the day, to watch the iron-red waters piling up against the *Wiggle*'s bows, to feel the cool breezes that swept down from the far-away mountains, and all this without being under the necessity of making conversation with Bones.

That gentleman had a no less profitable morning, for Ali Abid was a methodical and clerkly man, and unearthed the missing thirty-nine dollars in the Compensation Record.

"Thank goodness!" said Bones, relieved. "You're a jolly old accountant, Ali. I'd never have found it."

"Sir," said Ali, "some subjects, by impetuous application, omit vision of intricate detail. This is due to subjects' lack of concentration."

"Have it our way," said Bones, "but get the statement out for me to copy."

He awoke the girl from a profound reverie – which centred about shy and solemn bachelors who adopted whole nations of murderous children as their own – and proceeded to "take charge."

This implied the noisy issuing of orders which nobody carried out, the manipulation of a telescope, anxious glances at the heavens, deep and penetrating scrutinies at the water, and a promenade back and forward from one side of the launch to the other. Bones called this "pacing the bridge," and invariably carried his telescope tucked under his arm in the process, and, as he had to step over Pat's feet every time, and sometimes didn't, she arrested his nautical wanderings.

"You make me dizzy," she said. "And isn't that the island?"

In the early hours of the afternoon they re-embarked, the *capita* of the village coming to the beach to see them off.

They brought back with them a collection of spear-heads, gruesome execution knives, elephant swords, and wonderworking steel figures.

"And the lunch was simply lovely, Bones," agreed the girl, as the *Wiggle* turned her nose homeward. "Really, you can be quite clever sometimes."

"Dear old Miss Hamilton," said Bones, "you saw me today as I really am. The mask was off, and the real Bones, kindly, thoughtful, considerate, an' – if I may use the word without your foundin' any great hope upon it – tender. You saw me free from carkin' care, alert – "

"Go along and finish your accounts, like a good boy," she said. "I'm going to doze."

Doze she did, for it was a warm, dozy afternoon, and the boat was running swiftly and smoothly with the tide. Bones yawned and wrote, copying Ali's elaborate and accurate statement, whilst Ali himself slept contentedly on the top of the cabin. Even the engineer dozed at his post, and only one man was wide awake and watchful – Yoka, whose hands turned the wheel mechanically, whose dark eyes never left the river ahead, with its shoals, its sandbanks, and its snags, known and unknown.

Two miles from headquarters, where the river broadens before it makes its sweep to the sea, there are three islands with narrow passages between. At this season only one such passage – the centre of all – is safe. This is known as "The Passage of the Tree," because all boats, even the *Zaire*, must pass so close beneath the overhanging boughs of a great lime that the boughs brush their very funnels. Fortunately, the current is never strong here, for the passage is a shallow one. Yoka felt the boat slowing as he reached shoal water, and brought her nearer to the bank of the island. He had reached the great tree, when a noose dropped over him, tightened about his arms, and, before he could do more than lock the wheel, he was jerked from the boat and left swinging between bough and water.

"O Yoka," chuckled a voice from the bough, "between sunrise and moonset is no long time for a man to be with his wife!"

Bones had finished his account, and was thinking. He thought with his head on his hands, with his eyes shut, and his mouth open, and his thought was accompanied by strange guttural noises.

Patricia Hamilton was also thinking, but much more gracefully. Boosoobi sat by his furnace door, nodding. Sometimes he looked at the steam gauge, sometimes he kicked open the furnace door and chucked in a few billets of wood, but, in the main, he was listening to the soothing "chook-a-chook, chook-a-chook" of his well-oiled engines.

"Woo-yow!" yawned Bones, stretching himself, and came blinking into the sunlight. The sun was nearly setting.

"What the dooce – " said Bones. He stared round.

The *Wiggle* had run out from the mouth of the river and was at sea. There was no sign of land of any description. The low-lying shore of the territory had long since gone under the horizon.

Bones laid his hand on the shoulder of the sleeping girl, and she woke with a start.

"Dear old shipmate," he said, and his voice trembled, "we're alone on this jolly old ocean! Lost the steersman!"

She realized the seriousness of the situation in a moment.

The dozing engineer, now wide awake, came aft at Bones' call, and accepted the disappearance of the steersman without astonishment.

"We'll have to go back," said Bones, as he swung the wheel round. "I don't think I'm wrong in sayin' that the east is opposite to the west, an', if that's true, we ought to be home in time for dinner."

"Sar," said Boosoobi, who, being a coast boy, elected to speak English, "dem wood she no lib."

"Hey?" gasped Bones, turning pale.

"Dem wood she be done. I look um. I see um. I no find um."

Bones sat down heavily on the rail.

"What does he say?" Pat asked anxiously.

"He says there's no more wood," said Bones. "The horrid old bunkers are empty, an' we're at the mercy of the tempest."

"Oh, Bones!" she cried in consternation.

But Bones had recovered.

"What about swimmin' to shore with a line?" he said. "It can't be more than ten miles!"

It was Ali Abid who prevented the drastic step.

"Sir," he said, "the subject on such occasions should act with deliberate reserve. Proximity of land presupposes research. The subject should assist rather than retard research by passivity of action, easy respiration, and general normality of temperature."

"Which means, dear old Miss Hamilton, that you've got to keep your wool on," explained Bones.

What might have happened is not to be recorded, for at that precise moment the SS *Paretta* came barging up over the horizon.

There was still steam in the *Wiggle's* little boiler, and one log of wood to keep it at pressure.

Bones was incoherent, but again Ali came to the rescue.

"Sir," he said, "for intimating SOS-ness there is upon steamer or launch certain scientific apparatus, unadjusted, but susceptible to treatment."

"The wireless!" spluttered Bones. "Good lor', the wireless!"

Twenty minutes later the *Wiggle* ran alongside the gangway of the SS *Paretta,* anticipating the arrival of the *Zaire* by half an hour.

The SS *Paretta* was at anchor when Sanders brought the *Zaire* to the scene.

He saw the *Wiggle* riding serenely by the side of the great ship, looking for all the world like a humming bird under the wings of an ostrich, and uttered a prayer of thankfulness.

"They're safe," he said to Hamilton. "O Yoka, take the *Zaire* to the other side of the big boat."

"Master, do we go back tonight to seek Ko-buru?" asked Yoka, who was bearing marks which indicated his strenuous experience, for he had fought his way clear of his captors, and had swum with the stream to headquarters.

"Tomorrow is also a day," quoth Sanders.

Hamilton was first on the deck of the SS *Paretta*, and found his sister and a debonair and complacent Bones waiting for him. With them was an officer whom Hamilton recognized.

"Company accounts all correct, sir," said Bones, "audited by the jolly old paymaster" – he saluted the other officer – "an' found correct, sir, thus anticipatin' all your morose an' savage criticisms."

Hamilton gripped his hand and grinned.

"Bones was really wonderful," said the girl, "they wouldn't have seen us if it hadn't been for his idea."

"Saved by wireless, sir," said Bones nonchalantly. "It was a mere nothin' – just a flash of inspiration."

"You got the wireless to work?" asked Hamilton incredulously.

"No, sir," said Bones. "But I wanted a little extra steam to get up to the ship, so I burnt the dashed thing. I knew it would come in handy sooner or later."

# THE REMEDY

Beyond the far hills, which no man of the Ochori passed, was a range of blue mountains, and behind this again was the L'Mandi country. This adventurous hunting men of the Ochori had seen, standing in a safe place on the edge of the Great King's country. Also N'gombi people, who are notoriously disrespectful of all ghosts save their own, had, upon a time, penetrated the northern forest to a high knoll which Nature had shaped to the resemblance of a hayrick.

A huntsman climbing this after his lawful quarry might gain a nearer view of the blue mountains, all streaked with silver at certain periods of the year, when a hundred streams came leaping with feathery feet from crag to crag to strengthen the forces of the upper river, or, as some said, to create through underground channels the big lakes M'soobo and T'sambi at the back of the N'gombi country.

And on summer nights, when the big yellow moon came up and showed all things in her own chaste way, you might see from the knoll of the hayrick these silver ribbons all aglitter, though the bulk of the mountain was lost to sight.

The river folk saw little of the L'Mandi, because L'Mandi territory lies behind the country of the Great King, who looked with a jealous eye upon comings and goings in his land, and severely restricted the movement and the communications of his own people.

The great King followed his uncle in the government of the pleasant O'Mongo lands, and he had certain advantages and privileges, the significance of which he very imperfectly interpreted.

His uncle had died suddenly at the hands of Mr Commissioner Sanders, CMG, and the land itself might have passed into the protection of the Crown, for there was gold in the country in large and payable quantities.

That such a movement was arrested was due largely to the L'Mandi and the influence they were able to exercise upon the European Powers by virtue of their military qualities. Downing Street was all for a permanent occupation of the chief city and the institution of a conventional *régime*; but the L'Mandi snarled, clicked their heels, and made jingling noises with their great swords, and there was at that moment a government in office in England which was rather impressed by heel-clicking and sword-jingling, and so the territory of the Great King was left intact, and was marked on all maps as Omongoland, and coloured red, as being within the sphere of British influence. On the other hand, the L'Mandi people had it tinted yellow, and described it as an integral portion of the German Colonial Empire.

There was little communication between L'Mandi and Sanders' territory, but that little was more than enough for the Commissioner, since it took the shape of evangelical incursions carried out by missionaries who were in the happy position of not being obliged to say as much as "By your leave," since they had secured from a Government which was, as I say, impressed by heel-clicking and sword-jingling, an impressive document, charging "all commissioners, sub-commissioners, magistrates, and officers commanding our native forces," to give facilities to these good Christian gentlemen.

There were missionaries in the Territories who looked askance at their brethren, and Ferguson, of the River Mission, made a journey to headquarters to lay his views upon the subject before the Commissioner.

"These fellows aren't missionaries at all, Mr Sanders; they are just political agents utilizing sacred symbols to further a political propaganda."

"That is a Government palaver," smiled Sanders, and that was all the satisfaction Ferguson received. Nevertheless, Sanders was watchful, for there were times when the L'Mandi missioners and their friends strayed outside their sphere.

Once the L'Mandi folk had landed in a village in the middle Ochori, had flogged the headman, and made themselves free of the commodities which the people of the village had put aside for the payment of their taxation.

In his wrath, Bosambo, the chief, had taken ten war canoes; but Sanders, who had been in the Akasava on a shooting trip, was there before him, and had meted out swift justice to the evil-doers.

"And let me tell you, Bosambo," said Sanders severely, "that you shall not bring spears except at my word."

"Lord," said Bosambo, frankness itself, "if I disobeyed you, it was because I was too hot to think."

Sanders nodded.

"That I know," he said. "Now I tell you this, Bosambo, and this is the way of very wise men – that when they go to do evil things with a hot heart, they first sleep, and in their sleep their spirits go free and talk with the wise and the dead, and when they wake, their hearts are cool, and they see all the folly of the night, and their eyes are bright for their own faults."

"Master," said Bosambo, "you are my father and my mother, and all the people of the river you carry in your arms. Now I say to you that when I go to do an evil thing I will first sleep, and I will make all my people sleep also."

There are strange stories in circulation as to the manner in which Bosambo carried out this novel reform. There is the story of an Ochori wife-beater who, adjured by his chief, retired to slumber on his grievance, and came to his master the following morning with the information that he had not closed his eyes. Whereupon Bosambo clubbed him insensible, in order that Sanders' plan might have a fair chance.

At least, this is the story which Hamilton retailed at breakfast one morning. Sanders, appealed to for confirmation, admitted cautiously that he had heard the legend, but did not trouble to make an investigation.

"The art of governing a native country," he said, "is the art of not asking questions."

"But suppose you want to know something?" demanded Patricia.

"Then," said Sanders, with a twinkle in his eyes, "you must pretend. that you know."

"What is there to do today?" asked Hamilton, rolling his serviette.

He addressed himself to Lieutenant Tibbetts, who, to Sanders' intense annoyance, invariably made elaborate notes of all the Commissioner said.

"Nothin' until this afternoon, sir," said Bones, closing his note-book briskly, "then we're doin' a little deep-sea fishin'."

The girl made a grimace.

"We didn't catch anything yesterday, Bones," she objected.

"We used the wrong kind of worm," said Bones confidently. "I'ver found a new worm nest in the plantation. Jolly little fellers they are, too."

"What are we doing today, Bones?" repeated Hamilton ominously.

Bones puckered his brows.

"Deep-sea fishin', dear old officer and comrade," he repeated, "an' after dinner a little game of tiddly-winks – Bones *v.* jolly old Hamilton's sister, for the championship of the River an' the Sanders Cup."

Hamilton breathed deeply, but was patient.

"Your King and your country," he said, "pay you seven and eight-pence per diem – "

"Oh," said Bones, a light dawning, "you mean *work*?"

"Strange, is it not," mused Hamilton, "that we should consider – Hullo!"

They followed the direction of his eyes.

A white bird was circling groggily above the plantation, as though uncertain where to alight. There was weariness in the beat of its wings, in the irregularity of its flight. Bones lept over the rail of the verandah and ran towards the square. He slowed down as he came to a place beneath the bird, and whistled softly.

Bones' whistle was a thing of remarkable sweetness – it was his one accomplishment, according to Hamilton, and had neither tune nor rhyme. It was a succession of trills, rising and falling, and presently, after two hesitating swoops, the bird rested on his outstretched hand. He came back to the verandah and handed the pigeon to Sanders.

The Commissioner lifted the bird and with gentle fingers removed the slip of thin paper fastened to its leg by a rubber band.

Before he opened the paper he handed the weary little servant of the Government to an orderly.

"Lord, this is Sombubo," said Abiboo, and he lifted the pigeon to his cheek, "and he comes from the Ochori."

Sanders had recognized the bird, for Sombubo was the swiftest, the wisest, and the strongest of all his messengers, and was never dispatched except on the most critical occasions.

He smoothed the paper and read the letter, which was in Arabic.

From the servant of God Bosambo, in the Ochori City, to Sandi, where-the-sea-runs.

There have come three white men from the L'Mandi country, and they have crossed the mountains. They sit with the Akasava in full palaver. They say there shall be no more taxes for the People of the River, but there shall come a new king greater than any. And every man shall have goats and salt and free hunting. They say the Akasava shall be given all the Ochori country, also guns like the white man. Many guns and a thousand carriers are in the mountains waiting to come. I hold the Ochori with all my spears. Also the Isisi chief calls his young men for your King.

Peace be on your house in the name of Allah Compassionate and Merciful.

"M-m!" said Sanders, as he folded the paper. "I'm afraid there will be no fishing this afternoon. Bones, take the *Wiggle* and get up to the Akasava as fast as you can; I will follow on the *Zaire*. Abiboo!"

"Lord?"

"You will find me a swift Ochori pigeon. Hamilton, scribble a line to Bosambo, and say that he shall meet Bones by Sokala's village."

Half an hour later Bones was sending incomprehensible semaphore signals of farewell as the *Wiggle* slipped round the bend of the river.

Sokala, a little chief of the Isisi, was a rich man. He had ten wives, each of whom lived in her own hut. Also each wife wore about her neck a great ring of brass weighing twenty pounds, to testify to the greatness and wealth of her lord.

Sokala was wizened and lined of face, and across his forehead were many deep furrows, and it seemed that he lived in a state of perplexity as to what should become of all his riches when he died, for he was cursed with ten daughters – O'femi, Jubasami, K'sola, M'kema, Wasonga, Mombari, et cetera.

When Wasonga was fourteen, there was revealed to Sokala, her father, a great wonder.

The vision came at the tail end of a year of illness, when his head had ached for weeks together, and not even the brass wire twisted lightly about his skull brought him relief.

Sokala was lying on his fine bed of skins, wondering why strange animals sat by the fire in the centre of his hut, and why they showed their teeth and talked in human language. Sometimes they were leopards, sometimes they were little white-whiskered monkeys that scratched and told one another stories, and these monkeys were the wisest of all, for they discussed matters which were of urgency to the sick man rolling restlessly from side to side.

On this great night two such animals had appeared suddenly, a big grey fellow with a solemn face, and a very little one, and they sat staring into the fire, mechanically seeking their fleas until the little one spoke.

"Sokala is very rich and has ten daughters."

"That is true," said the other; "also he will die because he has no son."

Sokala's heart beat furiously with fear, but he listened when the little black monkey spoke.

"If Sokala took Wasonga, his daughter, into the forest near to The Tree and slew her, his daughters would become sons and he would grow well."

And the other monkey nodded.

As they talked, Sokala recognized the truth of all that they had said. He wondered that he had never thought of the matter before in this way. All night long he lay thinking – thinking – long after the fires had died down to a full red glow amidst white ashes, and the monkeys had vanished. In the cold dawn his people found him sitting on the side of the bed, and marvelled that he should have lived the night through.

"Send me Wasonga, my daughter," he said, and they brought a sleepy girl of fourteen, tall, straight and wholly reluctant. "We go a journey," said Sokala, and took from beneath his bed his wicker shield and his sharp-edged throwing-spear.

"Sokala hunts," said the people of the village significantly, and they knew that the end was very near, for he had been a great hunter, and men turn in death to the familiar pursuits of life.

Three miles on the forest road to the Isisi city, Sokala bade his daughter sit on the ground.

Bones had met and was in earnest conversation with the Chief of the Ochori, the *Wiggle* being tied up at a wooding, when he heard a scream, and saw a girl racing through the wood towards him.

Behind her, with the foolish stare on his face which comes to men in the last stages of sleeping sickness, his spear balanced, came Sokala.

The girl tumbled in a wailing, choking heap at Bones' feet, and her pursuer checked at the sight of the white man.

"I see you, Sokala,"* said Bones gently.

"Lord," said the old man, blinking at the officer of the Houssas, "you shall see a wonderful magic when I slay this woman, for my daughters shall be sons, and I shall be a well man."

Bones took the spear from his unresisting hand.

* The native equivalent for "Good morning."

71

"I will show you a greater magic, Sokala, for I will give you a little white stone which will melt like salt in your mouth, and you shall sleep."

The old man peered from Lieutenant Tibbetts to the King of the Ochori. He watched Bones as he opened his medicine chest and shook out two little white pellets from a bottle marked "Veronal," and accepted them gratefully.

"God bless my life," cried Bones, "don't chew 'em, you dear old silly — swallow 'em!"

"Lord," said Sokala soberly, "they have a beautiful and a magic taste."

Bones sent the frightened girl back to the village, and made the old man sit by a tree.

"O Tibbetti," said Bosambo, in admiration, "that was a good palaver. For it is better than the letting of blood, and no one will know that Sokala did not die in his time."

Bones looked at him in horror.

"Goodness gracious heavens, Bosambo," he gasped, "you don't think I've poisoned him?"

"Master," said Bosambo, nodding his head, "he die one time — he not fit for lib — you give um plenty no-good stuff. You be fine Christian feller same like me."

Bones wiped the perspiration from his brow and explained the action of veronal. Bosambo was sceptical. Even when Sokala fell into a profound slumber, Bosambo waited expectantly for his death. And when he realized that Bones had spoken the truth, he was a most amazed man.

"Master," he said, in that fluid Ochori dialect which seems to be made up of vowels, "this is a great magic. Now I see very surely that you hold wonderful ju-jus, and I have wronged you, for I thought you were without wisdom."

"Cheer-oh!" said the gratified Bones.

Near by the city of the Akasava is a small hill on which no vegetation grows, though it rises from a veritable jungle of undergrowth. The

Akasava call this place the Hill of the Women, because it was here that M'lama, the King of the Akasava, slew a hundred Akasava maidens to propitiate M'shimba M'shamba, the god of storms. It was on the topmost point of the hill that Sanders erected a fine gallows and hung M'lama for his country's good. It had always been associated with the spiritual history of the Akasava, for ghosts and devils and strange ju-jus had their home hereabouts, and every great decision at which the people arrived was made upon its slopes. At the crest was a palaver house – no more than a straw-thatched canopy affording shelter for four men at the most.

On a certain afternoon all the chiefs, great and minor, the headmen, the warriors, and the leaders of fishing villages of the Akasava, squatted in a semicircle and listened to the oration of a bearded man, who spoke easily in the river dialect of the happy days which were coming to the people.

By his side were two other white men – a tall, clean-shaven man with spectacles, and a stouter man with a bristling white moustache.

Had the bearded man's address been in plain English, or even in plain German, and had it been delivered to European hearers accustomed to taking its religion in allegories and symbols, it would have been harmless. As it was, the illustrations and the imagery which the speaker employed had no other interpretation to the simple-minded Akasava than a purely material one.

"I speak for the Great King," said the orator, throwing out his arms, "a king who is more splendid than any. He has fierce and mighty armies that cover the land like ants. He holds thunder and lightning in his hand, and is greater than M'shimba M'shamba. He is the friend of the black man and the white, and will deliver you from all oppression. He will give you peace and full crops, and make you *capita* over your enemies. When he speaks, all other kings tremble. He is a great buffalo, and the pawing of his hoofs shakes the earth.

"This he says to you, the warrior people of the Akasava – "

The message was destined to be undelivered.

Heads began to turn, and there was a whisper of words. Some of the audience half rose, some on the outskirts of the gathering stole quietly away – the lesser chiefs were among these – and others, sitting stolidly on, assumed a blandness and a scepticism of demeanour calculated to meet the needs of the occasion.

For Sanders was at the foot of the hill, a trim figure in white, his solar helmet pushed back to cover the nape of his neck from the slanting rays of the sun, and behind Sanders were two white officers and a company of Houssas with fixed bayonets. Not a word said Sanders, but slowly mounted the Hill of the Dead. He reached the palaver house and turned.

"Let no man go," he said, observing the disposition of the gathering to melt away, "for this is a great palaver, and I come to speak for these God-men."

The bearded orator glared at the Commissioner and half turned to his companions. The stout man with the moustache said something quickly, but Sanders silenced him with a gesture.

"O people," said Sanders, "you all know that under my King men may live in peace, and death comes quickly to those who make war. Also you may worship in what manner you desire, though it be my God or the famous gods of your fathers. And such as preach of God or gods have full liberty. Who denies this?"

"Lord, you speak the truth," said an eager headman.

"Therefore," said Sanders, "my King has given these God-men a book* that they may speak to you, and they have spoken. Of a great king they tell. Also of wonders which will come to you if you obey him. But this king is the same king of whom the God-cross men and the water-God men tell. For he lives beyond the stars, and his name is God. Tell me, preacher, is this the truth?"

The bearded man swallowed something and muttered, "This is true."

"Also, there is no king in this world greater than my King, whom you serve," Sanders continued, "and it is your duty to be obedient to him, and his name is D'jorja." Sanders raised his hand to his helmet in salute. "This also the God-men will tell you."

* A book = writen permission, any kind of document or writing.

He turned to the three evangelists.

Herr Professor Wiessmann hesitated for the fraction of a second. The pause was pardonable, for he saw the undoing of three months' good work, and his thoughts at that moment were with a certain party of carriers who waited in the mountains.

"The question of earthly and heavenly domination is always debatable," he began in English, but Sanders stopped him.

"We will speak in the Akasava tongue," he said, "and let all men hear. Tell me, shall my people serve my King, or shall they serve another?"

"They shall serve your King," growled the man, "for it is the law."

"Thank you," said Sanders in English.

The gathering slowly dispersed, leaving only the white men on the hill and a few lingering folk at the foot, watching the stolid native soldiery with an apprehension born of experience.

"We should like you to dine with us," said Sanders pleasantly.

The leader of the L'Mandi mission hesitated, but the thin man with the spectacles, who had been silent, answered for him.

"We shall be pleased, Mr Commissioner," he said. "After eating with these swine for a month, a good dinner would be very acceptable."

Sanders said nothing, though he winced at the inelegant description of his people, and the three evangelists went back to their huts, which had been built for their use by the Akasava chief.

An hour later that worthy sent for a certain witch-doctor.

"Go secretly," he said, "and call all headmen and chiefs to the Breaking Tree in the forest. There they shall be until the moon comes up, and the L'Mandi lords will come and speak freely. And you shall tell them that the word he spoke before Sandi was no true word, but to-night he shall speak the truth, and when Sandi is gone we shall have wonderful guns and destroy all who oppose us."

This the witch-doctor did, and came back by the river path.

Here, by all accounts, he met Bosambo, and would have passed on; but the chief of the Ochori, being in a curious mind and being, moreover, suspicious, was impressed by the importance of the messenger, and made inquiries…

An old man is a great lover of life, and after the witchdoctor's head had been twice held under water – for the river was providentially near – he gasped the truth.

The three missioners were very grateful guests indeed. They were the more grateful because Patricia Hamilton was an unexpected hostess. They clicked their heels and kissed her hand and drank her health many times in good hock. The dinner was a feast worthy of Lucullus, they swore, the wine was perfect, and the coffee – which Abiboo handed round with a solemn face – was wonderful.

They sat chatting for a time, and then the bearded man, looked at his watch.

"To bed, gentlemen," he said gaily. "We leave you, Herr Commissioner, in good friendship, we trust?"

"Oh, most excellent," said Sanders awkwardly, for he was a poor liar, and knew that his spies were waiting on the bank to "pick up" these potential enemies of his.

He watched them go ashore and disappear into the darkness of the forest path that leads to the village.

The moon was rising over the tall trees, and an expectant gathering of Akasava notables were waiting for a white spokesman who came not, when Bosambo and his bodyguard were engaged in lifting three unconscious men and laying them in a large canoe. He himself paddled the long boat to midstream, where two currents run swiftly, one to the sea and one to the Isisi River, which winds for a hundred miles until it joins the Congo.

"Go with God," said Bosambo piously, as he stepped into his own canoe, and released his hold of the other with its slumbering freight, "for if your king is so great, he will bring you to your own lands; and if he is not great, then you are liars. O Abiboo" – he spoke over his shoulder to the sergeant of Houssas – "tell me, how many of the magic white stones of Bonesi did you put in their drink?"

"Bosambo, I put four in each, as you told me, and if my lord Tibbetti misses them, what shall I say?"

"You shall say," said Bosambo, "that this is Sandi's own word – that when men plan evils they must first sleep. And I think these men will sleep for a long time. Perhaps they will sleep for ever – all things are with God."

# THE MEDICINE MAN

At the flood season, before the turbulent tributaries of the Isisi River had been induced to return to their accustomed channels, Sanders came back to headquarters a very weary man, for he had spent a horrid week in an endeavour – successful, but none the less nerve-racking – to impress an indolent people that the swamping of their villages was less a matter of Providence and ghosts than the neglect of elementary precaution.

"For I told you, Ranabini," said an exasperated Sanders, "that you should keep the upper channel free from trees and branches, and I have paid you many bags of salt for your services."

"Lord, it is so," said Ranabini, scratching his brown leg thoughtfully.

"At the full of the moon, before the rains, did I not ask you if the channel was clear, and did you not say it was like the street of your village?" demanded Sanders, in wrath.

"Lord," said Ranabini frankly, "I lied to you, thinking your lordship was mad. For what other man would foresee with his wonderful eye that rains would come? Therefore, lord, I did not think of the upper channel, and many trees floated down and made a little dam. Lord, I am an ignorant man, and my mind is full of my own brother, who has come from a long distance to see me, for he is a very sick man."

Sanders' mind was occupied by no thought of Ranabini's sick brother, as the dazzling white *Zaire* went thrashing her way down stream. For he himself was a tired man, and needed rest, and there was a dose of malaria looming in the offing, as his aching head told him.

It was as though his brains were arranged in slats, like a venetian blind, and these slats were opening and closing swiftly, bringing with each lightning flicker a momentary unconsciousness.

Captain Hamilton met him on the quay, and when Sanders landed – walking a thought unsteadily, and instantly began a long and disjointed account of his adventures on a Norwegian salmon river – Hamilton took him by the arm and led the way to the bungalow.

In ten minutes he was assisting Sanders into his pyjamas, Sanders protesting, albeit feebly, and when, after forcing an astonishing amount of quinine and arsenic down his chief's throat, Hamilton came from the semi-darkness of the bungalow to the white glare of the barrack square, Hamilton was thoughtful.

"Let one of your women watch by the bed of the lord Sandi," said he to Sergeant Abiboo, of the Houssas, "and she shall call me if he grows worse."

"On my life," said Abiboo, and was going off.

"Where is Tibbetti?" asked Hamilton.

The sergeant turned back and seemed embarrassed.

"Lord," he said, "Tibbetti has gone with the lady, your sister, to make a palaver with Jimbujini, the witch doctor of the Akasava. They sit in the forest in a magic circle, and lo! Tibbetti grows very wise."

Hamilton swore under his breath. He had ordered Lieutenant Tibbetts, his second-in-command, prop, stay, and aide-de-camp, to superintend the drill of some raw Kano recruits who had been sent from the coast.

"Go tell the lord Tibbetti to come to me," he said, "but first send your woman to Sandi."

Lieutenant: Tibbetts, with his plain, boyish-face all red with his exertions, yet dignified withal, came hurriedly from his studies.

"Come aboard, sir, he said, and saluted extravagantly, blinking at his superior with a curious solemnity of mien which was his own peculiar expression.

"Bones," said Hamilton, "where the dickens have you been?"

Bones drew a long breath. He hesitated, then – "Knowledge," he said shortly.

Hamilton looked at his subordinate in alarm.

"Dash it, you aren't off your head, too, are you?"

Bones shook his head with vigour.

"Knowledge of the occult, sir and brother-officer," he said. "One is never too old to learn, sir, in this jolly old world."

"Quite right," said Hamilton; "in fact, I'm pretty certain that you'll never live long enough to learn everything."

"Thank you, sir," said Bones.

The girl, who had less qualms than Bones when the summons arrived, and had, in consequence, returned more leisurely, came into the room.

"Pat," said her brother, "Sanders is down with fever."

"Fever!" she said a little breathlessly. "It isn't – dangerous?"

Bones, smiling indulgently, soothed her.

"Nothin' catchin', dear Miss Patricia Hamilton," he began.

"Please don't be stupid," she said so fiercely that Bones recoiled. "Do you think I'm afraid of catching anything? Is it dangerous for Mr Sanders?" she asked her brother.

"No more dangerous than a cold in the head," he answered flippantly. "My dear child, we all have fever. You'll have it, too, if you go out at sunset without your mosquito boots."

He explained, with the easy indifference of a man inured to malaria, the habits of the mosquito – his predilection for ankles and wrists, where the big veins and arteries are nearer to the surface – but the girl was not reassured. She would have sat up with Sanders, but the idea so alarmed Hamilton that she abandoned it.

"He'd never forgive me," he said. "My dear girl, he'll be as right as a trivet in the morning."

She was sceptical, but, to her amazement, Sanders turned up at breakfast his usual self, save that he was a little weary-eyed, and that his hand shook when he raised his coffee-cup to his lips. A miracle, thought Patricia Hamilton, and said so.

"Not at all, dear miss," said Bones, now as ever, accepting full credit for all phenomena she praised, whether natural or supernatural. "This is simply nothin' to what happened to me. Ham, dear old feller, do you remember when I was brought down from the Machengombi River? Simply delirious – ravin' – off my head."

"So much so," said Hamilton, slicing the top off his egg, "that we didn't think you were ill."

"If you'd seen me," Bones went on, solemnly shaking one skinny forefinger at the girl, "you'd have said: 'Bones is for the High Jump.' "

"I should have said nothing so vulgar, Bones," she retorted. "And was it malaria?"

"Ah," said Hamilton triumphantly, "I was too much of a gentleman to hint that it wasn't. Press the question, Pat."

Bones shrugged his shoulders and cast a look of withering contempt upon his superior.

"In the execution of one's duty, dear Miss Patricia H," he said, "the calibre of the gun that lays a fellow low, an' plunges his relations an' creditors into mournin', is beside the point. The only consideration, as dear old Omar says, is –

> '*The movin' finger hits, an', havin' hit,*
> *Moves on tum tumpty tumpty tay,*
> *And all a feller does won't make the slightest difference.*' "

"Is that Omar or Shakespeare?" asked the dazed Hamilton.

"Be quiet, dear. What was the illness, Bones?"

"Measles," said Hamilton brutally, "and German measles at that."

"Viciously put, dear old officer, but, nevertheless, true," said Bones buoyantly. "But when the hut's finished, I'll return good for evil. There's goin' to be a revolution, Miss Patricia Hamilton. No more fever, no more measles – health, wealth, an' wisdom, by gad!"

"Sunstroke," diagnosed Hamilton. "Pull yourself together, Bones – you're amongst friends."

But Bones was superior to sarcasm.

There was a creature of Lieutenant Tibbetts a solemn, brown man, who possessed, in addition to a vocabulary borrowed from a departed professor of bacteriology, a rough working knowledge of the classics.

This man's name was, as I have already explained, Abid Ali or Ali Abid, and in him Bones discovered a treasure beyond price.

Bones had recently built himself a large square hut near the seashore – that is to say, he had, with the expenditure of a great amount of midnight oil, a pair of compasses, a box of paints, and a T-square, evolved a somewhat complicated plan whereon certain blue oblongs stood for windows, and certain red cones indicated doors. To this he had added an elevation in the severe Georgian style.

With his plan beautifully drawn to scale, with sectional diagrams and side elevations embellishing its margin, he had summoned Mojeri of the Lower Isisi, famous throughout the land as a builder of great houses, and to him he had entrusted the execution of his design.

"This you shall build for me, Mojeri," said Bones, sucking the end of his pencil and gazing lovingly at the plan outspread before him, "and you shall be famous all through the world. This room shall be twice as large as that, and you shall cunningly contrive a passage so that I may move from one room to the other, and none see me come or go. Also, this shall be my sleeping-place, and this a great room where I will practise powerful magics."

Mojeri took the plan in his hand and looked at it. He turned it upside down and looked at it that way. Then he looked at it sideways.

"Lord," said he, putting down the plan with a reverent hand, "all these wonders I shall remember."

"And did he?" asked Hamilton, when Bones described the interview.

Bones blinked and swallowed.

"He went away and built me a square hut – just a plain square hut. Mojeri is an ass, sir – a jolly old fraud an' humbug, sir. He – "

"Let me see the plan," said Hamilton, and his subordinate produced the cartridge paper.

"H'm!" said Hamilton, after a careful scrutiny. "Very pretty. But how did you get into your room?"

"Through the door, dear old officer," said the sarcastic Bones.

"I thought it might be through the roof," said Hamilton, "or possibly you made one of your famous dramatic entries through a star-trap in the floor –

> *'Who is it speaks in those sepulchral tones?*
> *It is the demon king – the grisly Bones! Bing!'*

and up you pop amidst red fire and smoke."

A light dawned on Bones.

"Do you mean to tell me, jolly old Ham, that I forgot to put a door into my room?" he asked incredulously, and peered over his chief's shoulder.

"That is what I mean, Bones. And where does the passage lead to?"

"That goes straight from my sleepin' room to the room marked L," said Bones, in triumph.

"Then you *were* going to be a demon king," said the admiring Hamilton. "But fortunately for you, Bones, the descent to L is not so easy – you've drawn a party wall across – "

"L stands for laboratory," explained the architect hurriedly. "An' where's the wall? God bless my jolly old soul, so I have! Anyway, that could have been rectified in a jiffy."

"Speaking largely," said Hamilton, after a careful scrutiny of the plan, "I think Mojeri has acted wisely. You will have to be content with one room. What was the general idea of the house, anyway?"

"Science an' general illumination of the human mind," said Bones comprehensively.

"I see," said Hamilton. "You were going to make fireworks. A splendid idea, Bones."

"Painful as it is to undeceive you, dear old sir," said Bones, with admirable patience, "I must tell you that I'm takin' up my medical studies where I left off. Recently I've been wastin' my time, sir: precious hours an' minutes have been passed in frivolous amusement – *tempus fugit*, sir an' captain, *festina lente*, an' I might add – "

"Don't," begged Hamilton; "you give me a headache."

There was a look of interest in Bones' eyes.

"If I may be allowed to prescribe, sir – " he began. "Thanks, I'd rather have the headache," replied Hamilton hastily.

It was nearly a week before the laboratory was fitted that Bones gave a house-warming, which took the shape of an afternoon tea. Bones, arrayed in a long white coat, wearing a ferocious lint mask attached to huge mica goggles, through which he glared on the world, met the party at the door and bade them a muffled welcome. They found the interior of the hut a somewhat uncomfortable place. The glass retorts, test tubes, bottles, and the paraphernalia of science which Bones had imported crowded the big table, the shelves, and even overflowed on to the three available chairs.

"Welcome to my little workroom," said the hollow voice of Bones from behind the mask. "Wel – Don't put your foot in the crucible, dear old officer! You're sittin' on the methylated spirits, ma'am! Phew!"

Bones removed his mask and showed a hot, red face.

"Don't take it off, Bones," begged Hamilton; "it improves you."

Sanders was examining the microscope, which stood under a big glass shade.

"You're very complete, Bones," he said approvingly. "In what branch of science are you dabbling?"

"Tropical diseases, sir," said Bones promptly, and lifted the shade. "I'm hopin' you'll allow me to have a look at your blood after tea."

"Thank you," said Sanders. "You had better practise on Hamilton."

"Don't come near me!" threatened Hamilton.

It was Patricia who, when the tea-things had been removed, played the heroine.

"Take mine," she said, and extended her hand.

Bones found a needle, and sterilized it in the flame of a spirit lamp.

"This won't hurt you," he quavered, and brought the point near the white firm flesh. Then he drew it back again.

"This won't hurt you, dear old miss," he croaked, and repeated the performance.

He stood up and wiped his streaming brow. "I haven't the heart to do it," he said dismally.

"A pretty fine doctor you are, Bones!" she scoffed, and took the needle from his hand. "There!"

Bones put the tiny crimson speck between his slides, blobbed a drop of oil on top, and focused the microscope.

He looked for a long time, then turned a scared face to the girl.

"Sleepin' sickness, poor dear old Miss Hamilton!" he gasped. "You're simply full of tryps! Good Lord! What a blessin' for you I discovered it!"

Sanders pushed the young scientist aside and looked. When he turned his head, the girl saw his face was white and drawn, and for a moment a sense of panic overcame her.

"You silly ass," growled the Commissioner, "they aren't trypanosomes! You haven't cleaned the infernal eyepiece!"

"Not trypanosomes?" said Bones.

"You seem disappointed, Bones," said Hamilton.

"As a man, I'm overjoyed," replied Bones gloomily; "as a scientist, it's a set-back, dear old officer – a distinct set-back."

The house-warming lasted a much shorter time than the host had intended. This was largely due to the failure of a very beautiful experiment which he had projected. In order that the rare and wonderful result at which he aimed should be achieved, Bones had the hut artificially darkened, and they sat in a dark and sticky blackness, whilst he knocked over bottles and swore softly at the instruments his groping hand could not discover. And the end of the experiment was a large, bad smell.

"The women and children first," said Hamilton, and dived for the door.

They took farewell of Bones at a respectful distance.

Hamilton went across to the Houssa lines, and Sanders walked back to the Residency with the girl. For a little while they spoke of Bones and his newest craze, and then suddenly the girl asked –

"You didn't really think there were any of those funny things in my blood, did you?"

Sanders looked straight ahead.

"I thought – you see, we know – the tryp is a distinct little body, and anybody who had lived in this part of the world for a time can pick him out. Bones, of course, knows nothing thoroughly – I should have remembered that."

She said nothing until they reached the verandah, and she turned to go to her room.

"It wasn't nice, was it?" she said.

Sanders shook his head.

"It was a taste of hell," he said simply. And she fetched a quick, long sigh and patted his arm before she realized what she was doing.

Bones, returning from his hut, met Sanders hurrying across the square.

"Bones, I want you to go up to the Isisi," said the Commissioner. "There's an outbreak of some weird disease, probably due to the damming of the little river by Ranabini, and the flooding of the low forests."

Bones brightened up.

"Sir an' Excellency," he said gratefully, "comin' from you, this tribute to my scientific – "

"Don't be an ass, Bones!" said Sanders irritably. "Your job is to make these beggars work. They'll simply sit and die unless you start them on drainage work. Cut a few ditches with a fall to the river; kick Ranabini for me; take up a few kilos of quinine and dose them."

Nevertheless, Bones managed to smuggle on board quite a respectable amount of scientific apparatus, and came in good heart to the despondent folk of the Lower Isisi.

Three weeks after Bones had taken his departure, Sanders was sitting at dinner in a very thoughtful mood.

Patricia had made several ineffectual attempts to draw him into a conversation, and had been answered in monosyllables. At first she had been piqued and a little angry, but, as the meal progressed, she realized that matters of more than ordinary seriousness were occupying his thoughts, and wisely changed her attitude of mind. A chance reference to Bones, however, succeeded where more pointed attempts had failed.

"Yes," said Sanders, in answer to the question she had put, "Bones has some rough idea of medical practice. He was a cub student at Bart's for two years before he realized that surgery and medicines weren't his forte."

"Don't you sometimes feel the need of a doctor here?" she asked, and Sanders smiled.

"There is very little necessity. The military doctor comes down occasionally from headquarters, and we have a native apothecary. We have few epidemics amongst the natives, and those the medical missions deal with – sleep – sickness, beri-beri and the like. Sometimes, of course, we have a pretty bad outbreak which spreads – Don't go, Hamilton – I want to see you for a minute."

Hamilton had risen, and was making for his room, with a little nod to his sister.

At Sanders' word he turned.

"Walk with me for a few minutes," said Sanders, and, with an apology to the girl he followed the other from the room.

"What is it?" asked Hamilton.

Sanders was perturbed – this he knew, and his own move towards his room was in the nature of a challenge for information.

"Bones," said the Commissioner shortly. "Do you realize that we have had no news from him since he left?"

Hamilton smiled.

"He's an erratic beggar, but nothing could have happened to him, or we should have heard about it."

Sanders did not reply at once. He paced up and down the gravelled path before the Residency, his hands behind him.

"No news has come from Ranabini's village for the simple reason that nobody has entered or left it since Bones arrived," he said. "It is situated, as you know, on a tongue of land at the confluence of two rivers. No boat has left the beaches, and an attempt to reach it by land has been prevented by force."

"By force?" repeated the startled Hamilton.

Sanders nodded.

"I had a report in this morning. Two men of the Isisi from another village went to call on some relations. They were greeted with arrows, and returned hurriedly. The headman of M'gomo village met with the same reception. This came to the ears of my chief spy Ahmet, who attempted to paddle to the island in his canoe. At a distance of two hundred yards he was fired upon."

"Then they've got Bones?" gasped Hamilton.

"On the contrary, Bones nearly got Ahmet, for Bones was the marksman."

The two men paced the path in silence.

"Either Bones has gone mad," said Hamilton, "or – "

"Or – ?"

Hamilton laughed helplessly.

"I can't fathom the mystery," he said. "McMasters will be down tomorrow, to look at some sick men. We'll take him up, and examine the boy."

It was a subdued little party that boarded the *Zaire* the following morning, and Patricia Hamilton, who came to see them off, watched their departure with a sense of impending trouble.

Dr McMasters alone was cheerful, for this excursion represented a break in a somewhat monotonous routine.

"It may be the sun," he suggested. "I have known several fellows who have gone a little nutty from that cause. I remember a man at Grand Bassam who shot – "

"Oh, shut up, Mac, you grisly devil!" snapped Hamilton. "Talk about butterflies."

The *Zaire* swung round the bend of the river that hid Ranabini's village from view, but had scarcely come into sight when –

"Ping!"

Sanders saw the bullet strike the river ahead of the boat, and send a spiral column of water shooting into the air. He put up his glasses and focused them on the village beach.

"Bones!" he said grimly. "Take her in, Abiboo."

As the steersman spun the wheel –

"Ping!"

This time the shot fell to the right.

The three white men looked at one another.

"Let every man take cover," said Sanders quietly. "We're going to that beach even if Bones has a battery of 75's!"

An exclamation from Hamilton arrested him. "He's signalling," said the Houssa Captain, and Sanders put up the glasses again.

Bones' long arms were waving at ungainly angles as he semaphored his warning.

Hamilton opened his notebook and jotted down the message – "Awfully sorry, dear old officer," he spelt, and grinned at the unnecessary exertion of this fine preliminary flourish, "but must keep you away. Bad outbreak of virulent smallpox – "

Sanders whistled, and pulled back the handle of the engine-room telegraph to "stop."

"My God!" said Hamilton through his teeth, for he had seen such an outbreak once, and knew something of its horrors. Whole districts had been devastated in a night. One tribe had been wiped out, and the rotting frames of their houses still showed amidst the tangle of elephant grass which had grown up through the ruins.

He wiped his forehead and read the message a little unsteadily, for his mind was on his sister –

"Had devil of fight, and lost twenty men, but got it under. Come and get me in three weeks. Had to stay here for fear of careless devils spreading disease."

Sanders looked at Hamilton, and McMasters chuckled.

"This is where I get a swift vacation," he said, and called his servant.

Hamilton leapt on to the rail, and steadying himself against a stanchion, waved a reply – "We are sending you a doctor."

Back came the reply in agitated sweeps of arm – "Doctor be blowed! What am I?"

"What shall I say, sir?" asked Hamilton after he had delivered the message.

"Just say 'a hero,' " said Sanders huskily.

# BONES, KING-MAKER

Patricia Hamilton, an observant young lady, had not failed to notice that every day, at a certain hour, Bones, disappeared from view. It was not for a long time that she sought an explanation.

"Where is Bones?" she asked one morning, when the absence of her cavalier was unusually protracted.

"With his baby," said her brother.

"Please don't be comic, dear. Where *is* Bones? I thought I saw him with the ship's doctor."

The mail had come in that morning, and the captain and surgeon of the SS *Boma Queen* had been their guests at breakfast.

Hamilton looked up from his book and removed his pipe.

"Do you mean to tell me that Bones has kept his guilty secret all this time?" he asked anxiously.

She sat down by his side.

"Please tell me the joke. This isn't the first time you have ragged Bones about 'the baby'; even Mr Sanders has done it."

Sho looked across at the Commissioner with a reproving shake of her pretty head.

"Have I ragged Bones?" asked Sanders, in surprise. "I never thought I was capable of ragging anybody."

"The truth is, Pat," said her brother, "there isn't any rag about the matter. Bones adopted a piccanin."

"A child?"

"A baby about a month old. Its mother died, and some old bird of a witch-doctor was 'chopping' it when Bones appeared on the scene."

Patricia gave a little gurgle of delight and clapped her hands. "Oh, please tell me everything about it."

It was Sanders who told her of Henry Hamilton Bones, his dire peril and his rescue; it was Hamilton who embellished the story of how Bones had given his adopted son his first bath.

"Just dropped him into a tub and stirred him round with a mop."

Soon after this Bones came blithely up from the beach and across the parade-ground, his large pipe in his mouth, his cane awhirl.

Hamilton watched him from the verandah of the Residency, and called over his shoulder to Patricia.

It had been an anxious morning for Bones, and even Hamilton was compelled to confess to himself that he had felt the strain, though he had not mentioned the fact to his sister.

Outside in the roadstead the intermediate Elder Dempster boat was waiting the return of the doctor. Bones had been to see him off. An important day, indeed, for Henry Hamilton Bones had been vaccinated.

"I think it 'took,'" said Bones gravely, answering the other's question. "I must say Henry behaved like a gentleman."

"What did Fitz say?"

(Fitzgerald, the doctor, had come in accordance with his promise to perform the operation.)

"Fitz?" said Bones, and his voice trembled. "Fitz is a cad!"

Hamilton grinned.

"He said that babies didn't feel pain, and there was Henry howling his young head off. It was horrible!"

Bones wiped his streaming brow with a large and violent bandana, and looked round cautiously.

"Not a word, Ham, to her!" he said, in a loud whisper.

"Sorry!" said Hamilton, picking up his pipe. "Her knows."

"Good gad!" said Bones, in despair, and turned to meet the girl.

"Oh, Bones! she said reproachfully, "You never told me!"

Bones shrugged his shoulders, opened his mouth, dropped his pipe, blinked, spread out his hands in deprecation, and picked up his pipe.

From which it may be gathered that he was agitated.

"Dear old Miss Hamilton," he said tremulously, "I should be a horrid bounder if I denied Henry Hamilton Bones – poor little chap. If I never mentioned him, dear old sister, it is because – Ah, well, you will never understand."

He hunched his shoulders dejectedly.

"Don't be an ass, Bones. Why the dickens are you making a mystery of the thing?" asked Hamilton. "I'll certify you're a jolly good father to the brat."

"Not 'brat,' dear old sir," begged Bones. "Henry is a human being with a human heart. That boy" – he wagged his finger solemnly – "knows me the moment I go into the hut. To see him sit up an' say 'Da!' dear old sister Hamilton," he went on incoherently, "to see him open his mouth with a smile, one tooth through, an' one you can feel with your little finger – why, it's – it's wonderful, jolly old Miss Hamilton! Damn it, it's wonderful! "

"Bones!" cried the shocked girl.

"I can't help it, madame," said Bones miserably. "Fitz cut his poor little, fat little arm. Oh, Fitz is a low cad! Cut it, my dear old Patricia, mercilessly – yes, mercilessly, brutally, an' the precious little blighter didn't so much as call for the police. Good gad, it was terrible!"

His eyes were moist, and he blew his nose with great vigour.

"I'm sure it was awful," she soothed him. "May I come and see him?"

Bones raised a warning hand, and, though the habitat of the wonderful child could not have been less than half a mile away, lowered his voice.

"He's asleep – fitfully, but asleep. I've told them to call me if he has a turn for the worse, an' I'm goin' down with a gramophone after dinner, in case the old fellow wants buckin' up. But now he's asleep, thankin' you for your great kindness an' sympathy, dear old miss, in the moment of singular trial."

He took her hand and shook it heartily, tried to say something, and swallowed hard, then, turning, walked from the verandah in the direction of his hut.

The girl was smiling, but there were tears in her eyes.

"What a boy!" she said, half to herself.

Sanders nodded.

"Bones is very nice," he said, and she looked at him curiously.

"That is most eloquent," she said quietly.

"I thought it was rather bald," he replied. "You see, few people really understand Bones. I thought, the first time I saw him, that he was a fool. I was wrong. Then I thought he was effeminate. I was wrong again, for he has played the man whenever he was called upon to do so. Bones is one of those rare creatures – a man with all the moral equipment of a good woman."

Her eyes were fixed on his, and for a moment they held. Then her eyes dropped quickly, and she flushed ever so slightly.

"I think you have defined the perfect man," she said, turning the leaves of her book.

The next morning she was admitted to an audience with that paragon of paragons, Henry Hamilton Bones.

He lived in the largest of the Houssa huts at the far end of the lines, and had for attendants two native women, for whom Bones had framed the most stringent and regimental of orders.

The girl paused in the porch of the hut to read the typed written regulations which were fastened by drawing-pins to a green baize board.

They were bi-lingual, being in English and in coast Arabic, in which dialect Bones was something of a master. The girl wondered why they should be in English.

"Absolutely necessary, dear old lady friend," explained Bones firmly. "You've no idea what a lot of anxiety I have had. Your dear old brother – God bless him! – is a topping old sport, but with children you can't be too careful, and Ham is awfully thoughtless. There, I've said it!"

The English part of the regulations was brief, and she read it through.

## HENRY HAMILTON BONES (Care of).

1. Visitors are requested to make as little noise as possible. How would you like to be awakened from refreshing sleep! Be unselfish, and put yourself in his place.

2. It is absolutely forbidden to feed the child except with articles a list of which may be obtained on application. Nuts and chocolates are strictly forbidden.

3. The undersigned will not be responsible for articles broken by the child, such as watches. If watches are used to amuse child, they should be held by child's ear, when an interested expression will be observed on child's face. On no account should child be allowed – knowing no better – to bite watch, owing to danger from glass, minute hand, etc.

4. In lifting child, grasp above waist under arms and raise slowly, taking care that head does not fall back. Bring child close to holder's body, passing left arm under child and right arm over. Child should not be encouraged to sit up – though quite able to, being very forward for eight months – owing to strain on back. On no account should child be thrown up in the air and caught.

5. Any further information can be obtained at Hut 7.

(Signed) AUGUSTUS TIBBETTS, Lieutenant.

"All based on my personal observation and experience," said Bones triumphantly – "not a single tip from anybody."

"I think you are really marvellous, Bones," said the girl, and meant it.

Henry Hamilton Bones sat upright in a wooden cot. A fat-faced atom of brown humanity, bald-headed and big-eyed, he sucked his thumb and stared at the visitor, and from the visitor to Bones.

Bones he regarded with an intelligent interest which dissolved into a fat chuckle of sheer delight.

"Isn't it – isn't it simply extraordinary?" demanded Bones ecstatically. "In all your long an' painful experience, dear old friend an' co-worker, have you ever seen anything like it? When you remember that babies don't open their eyes until three weeks after they're born – "

"Da!" said Henry Hamilton Bones.

"Da yourself, Henry!" squawked his foster-father.

"Do da!" said Henry.

The smile vanished from Bones' face, and he bit his lip thoughtfully.

"Do da!" he repeated. "Let me see, what is 'do da'?"

"Do da!" roared Henry.

"Dear old Miss Hamilton," he said gently, "I don't know whether Henry wants a drink or whether he has a pain in his stomach, but I think that we had better leave him in more experienced hands."

He nodded fiercely to the native woman nurse and made his exit.

Outside they heard Henry's lusty yell, and Bones put his hand to his ear and listened with a strained expression on his face.

Presently the tension passed.

"It *was* a drink," said Bones. "Excuse me whilst I make a note." He pulled out his pocket-book and wrote: " 'Do da' means 'child wants drink.'"

He walked back to the Residency with her, giving her a remarkable insight into Henry's vocabulary. It appeared that babies have a language of their own, which Bones boasted that he had almost mastered.

She lay awake for a very long time that night, thinking of Bones, his simplicity and his lovableness. She thought, too, of Sanders, grave, aloof, and a little shy, and wondered…

She woke with a start, to hear the voice of Bones outside the window. She felt sure that something had happened to Henry. Then she heard Sanders and her brother speaking, and realized that it was not Henry they were discussing.

She looked at her watch – it was three o'clock.

I was foolish to trust that fellow," Sanders was saying, "and I know that Bosambo is not to blame, because he has always given a very wide berth to the Kulumbini people, though they live on his border."

95

She heard him speak in a strange tongue to some unknown fourth, and guessed that a spy of the Government had come in during the night.

"We'll get away as quickly as we can, Bones," Sanders said. "We can take our chance with the lower river in the dark; it will be daylight before we reach the bad shoals. You need not come, Hamilton."

"Do you think Bones will be able to do all you want?" Hamilton's tone was dubious.

"Pull yourself together, dear old officer," said Bones raising his voice to an insubordinate pitch.

She heard the men move from the verandah, and fell asleep again, wondering who was the man they spoke of and what mischief he had been brewing.

On a little tributary stream, which is hidden by the island of bats, was the village of Kulumbini. High elephant grass hid the poor huts even from they who navigate a cautious way along the centre of the narrow stream. On the shelving beach one battered old canoe of ironwood, with its sides broken and rusted, the indolence of its proprietor made plain by the badly spliced panels, was all that told the stranger that the habitations of man were nigh.

Kulumbini was a term of reproach along the great river and amongst the people of the Akasava, the Isisi, and the N'gombi, no less than among that most tolerant of tribes the Ochori. They were savage people, immensely brave, terrible in battle, but more terrible after.

Kulumbini, the village and city of the tribe, was no more than an outlier of a fairly important tribe which occupied forest land stretching back to the Ochori boundary. Their territory knew no frontier save the frontiers of caprice and desire. They had neither nationality nor national ambition, and would sell their spears for a bunch of fish, as the saying goes. Their one consuming passion and one great wish was that they should not be overlooked, and, so long as the tribes respected this eccentricity, the Kulumbini distressed no man.

How this desire for isolation arose, none know. It is certain that once upon a time they possessed a king who so shared their views that he never came amongst them, but lived in a forest place which is called to this day S'furi-S'foosi, "The trees (or glade) of the distant king." They had demurred at Government inspection, and Sanders, coming up the little river on the first of his visits, was greeted by a shower of arrows, and his landing opposed by locked shields.

There are many ways of disposing of opposition, not the least important of which is to be found in two big brass-barrelled guns which have their abiding place at each end of the *Zaire*'s bridge. There is also a method known as peaceful suasion. Sanders had compromised by going ashore for a peace palaver with a revolver in each hand.

He had a whole fund of Bomongo stories, most of which are unfit for printing, but which, nevertheless, find favour amongst the primitive humorists of the Great River. By parable and story, by nonsense tale and romance, by drawing upon his imagination to supply himself with facts, by invoking ju-jus, ghosts, devils, and all the armoury of native superstition, he had, in those far-off times, prevailed upon the people of Kulumbini not only to allow him a peaceful entrance to their country, but – wonder of wonders! – to contribute, when the moon and tide were in certain relative positions, which in English means once every six months, a certain tithe or tax, which might consist of rubber, ivory, fish, or manioc, according to the circumstances of the people.

More than this, he stamped a solemn treaty – he wrote it in a tattered laundry-book which had come into the chief's possession by some mysterious means – and he hung about the neck of Gulabala, the titular lord of these strange people, the medal and chain of chieftainship.

Not to be outdone in courtesy, the chief offered him the choice of all the maidens of Kulumbini, and Sanders, to whom such offers were by no means novel, had got out of a delicate situation in his usual manner, having resort to witchcraft for the purpose. For he said, with due solemnity and hushed breath, that it had been predicted by a celebrated witch-doctor of the lower river that the next wife he should take to himself would die of sickness mongo, and said Sanders – "My heart is too tender for your people, O Chief, to lead one of your beautiful daughters to death."

"O Sandi," replied Gulabala hopefully, "I have many daughters, and I should not miss one. And would it not be good service for a woman of my house to die in your hut?"

"We see things differently, you and I," said Sanders, "for, according to my religion, if any woman dies from witchcraft, her ghost sits for ever at the foot of my bed, making terrifying faces."

Thus Sanders had made his escape, and had received at odd intervals the tribute of these remote people.

For years they had dwelt without interference, for they were an unlucky people to quarrel with, and, save for one or two trespasses on the part of Gulabala, there was no complaint made concerning them. It is not natural, however, for native people to prosper, as these folks did, without there growing up a desire to kill somebody. For does not the river saying run: "The last measure of a full granary is a measure of blood"?

In the dead of a night Gulabala took three hundred spears across the frontier to the Ochori village of Netcka, and returned at dawn with the spears all streaky. And he brought back with him some twenty women, who would have sung the death-song of their men but for the fact that Gulabala and his warriors beat them.

Gulabala slept all the day, he and his spears, and woke to a grisly vision of consequence.

He called his people together and spoke in this wise – "Soon Sandi and his headmen will come, and, if we are here, there will be many folk hanged, for Sandi is a cruel man. Therefore let us go to a far place in the forest, carrying our treasure, and when Sandi has forgiven us, we will come back."

A good plan but for the sad fact that Bosambo of the Ochori was less than fifty miles away at the dawn of that fatal day, and was marching swiftly to avenge his losses, for not only had Gulabala taken women, but he had taken sixty goats, and that was unpardonable.

The scouts which Gulabala had sent out came back with the news that the way to sanctuary was barred by Bosambo.

Now, of all the men that the Kulumbini hated, they hated none more than the Chief of the Ochori. For he alone never scrupled to overlook them, and to dare their anger by flogging such of them as raided his territory in search of game.

"Ko," said Gulabala, deeply concerned, "this Bosambo is Sandi's dog. Let us go back to our village and say we have been hunting, for Bosambo will not cross into our lands for fear of Sandi's anger."

They reached the village, and were preparing to remove the last evidence of their crime – one goat looks very much like another, but women can speak – when Sanders came striding down the village street, and Gulabala, with his curved execution knife in his hand, stood up by the side of the woman he had slain.

"O Gulabala," said Sanders softly, "this is an evil thing."

The chief looked left and right helplessly.

"Lord," he spoke huskily, "Bosambo and his people put me to shame, for they spied on me and overlooked me. And we are proud people, who must not be overlooked – thus it has been for all time."

Sanders pursed his lips and stared at the man.

"I see here a fine high tree," he said, "so high that he who hangs from its top branch may say that no man overlooks him. There you shall hang, Gulabala, for your proud men to see, before they also go to work for my King, with chains upon their legs as long as they live."

"Lord," said Gulabala philosophically, "I have lived."

Ten minutes later he went the swift way which bad chiefs go, and his people were unresentful spectators.

"This is the tenth time I have had to find a new chief in this belt," said Sanders, pacing the deck of the *Zaire*, "and who on earth I am to put in his place I do not know."

The *lokalis* of the Kolumbini were already calling headmen to grand palaver. In the shade of the reed-thatched *lokali* house, before the hollow length of tree-trunk, the player worked his flat drumsticks of ironwood with amazing rapidity. The call trilled and rumbled, rising and falling, now a patter of light musical sound, now a low grumble.

Bosambo came – by the river route – as Sanders was leaving the *Zaire* to attend the momentous council.

"How say you, Bosambo – what man of the Kulumbini folk will hold these people in check?"

Bosambo squatted at his lord's feet and set his spear a-spinning.

"Lord," he confessed, "I know of none, for they are a strange and hateful people. Whatever king you set above them they will despise. Also they worship no gods or ghosts, nor have they ju-ju or fetish. And, if a man does not believe, how may you believe him? Lord, this I say to you – set me above the Kulumbini, and I will change their hearts."

But Sanders shook his head.

"That may not be, Bosambo," he said.

The palaver was a long and weary one. There were twelve good claimants for the vacant stool of office, and behind the twelve there were kinsmen and spears.

From sunset to nigh on sunrise they debated the matter, and Sanders sat patiently through it all, awake and alert. Whether this might be said of Bones is questionable. Bones swears that he did not sleep, and spent the night, chin in hand, turning over the problem in his mind.

It is certain he was awake when Sanders gave his summing up.

"People of this land," said Sanders, "four fires have been burnt since we met, and I have listened to all your words. Now, you know how good it is that there should be one you call chief. Yet, if I take you, M'loomo" – he turned to one sullen claimant – "there will be war. And if I take B'songi, there will be killing. And I have come to this mind – that I will appoint a king over you who shall not dwell with you nor overlook you."

Two hundred pairs of eyes watched the Commissioner's face. He saw the gleam of satisfaction which came at this concession to the traditional characteristic of the tribe, and went on, almost completely sure of his ground.

"He shall dwell far away, and you, the twelve kinsmen of Gulabala, shall reign in his place – one at every noon shall sit in the chief's chair and keep the land for your king, who shall dwell with me."

One of the prospective regents rose.

"Lord, that is good talk, for so did Sakalaba, the great king of our race, live apart from us at S'furi-S'foosi, and were we not prosperous in those days? Now tell us what man you will set over us."

For one moment Sanders was nonplussed. He was rapidly reviewing the qualifications of all the little chiefs, the headmen, and the fisher leaders who sat under him, and none fulfilled his requirements.

In that moment of silence an agitated voice whispered in his ear, and Bones' lean hand clutched his sleeve.

"Sir an' Excellency," breathed Bones, all of a twitter, "don't think I'm takin' advantage of my position, but it's the chance I've been lookin' for, sir. You'd do me an awful favour – you see, sir, I've got his career to consider – "

"What on earth – " began Sanders.

"Henry Hamilton Bones, sir," said Bones tremulously. "You'd set him up for life, sir. I must think of the child, hang it all! I know I'm a jolly old rotter to put my spoke in – "

Sanders gently released the frenzied grip of his lieutenant, and faced the wondering palaver.

"Know all people that this day I give to you as king one whom you shall call M'songuri, which means in your tongue 'The Young and the Wise,' and who is called in my tongue N'risu M'ilitani Tibbetti, and this one is a child and well beloved by my lord Tibbetti, being to him as a son, and by M'ilitani and by me, Sandi."

He raised his hand in challenge.

"Wa! Whose men are you?" he cried.

"M'songuri!"

The answer came in a deep-throated growl, and the assembly leapt to its feet.

"Wa! Who rules this land?"

"M'songuri!"

They locked arms and stamped first with the right foot and then with the left, in token of their acceptance.

"Take your king," said Sanders, "and build him a beautiful hut, and his spirit shall dwell with you. This palaver is finished."

Bones was speechless all the way down river. At irregular intervals he would grip Sanders' hand, but he was too full for speech.

Hamilton and his sister met the law-givers on the quay.

"You're back sooner than I expected you, sir," said Hamilton. "Did Bones behave?"

"Like a little gentleman," said Sanders.

"Oh, Bones," Patricia broke in eagerly, "Henry has cut another tooth."

Bones' nod was grave and even distant.

"I will go and see His Majesty," he said. "I presume he is in the palace?"

Hamilton stared after him.

"Surely," he asked irritably, "Bones isn't sickening for measles again?"

# THE TAMER OF BEASTS

Native folk, at any rate, are but children of a larger growth. In the main, their delinquencies may be classified under the heading of "naughtiness." They are mischievous and passionate, and they have a weakness for destroying things to discover the secrets of volition. A too prosperous nation mystifies less fortunate people, who demand of their elders and rulers some solution of the mystery of their rivals' progress. Such a ruler, unable to offer the necessary explanation, takes his spears to the discovery, and sometimes discovers too much for his happiness.

The village of Jumburu stands on the edge of the bush country, where the lawless men of all nations dwell. This territory is filled with fierce communities, banded together against a common enemy – the law. They call this land the B'wigini, which means "the Nationless," and Jumburu's importance lies in the fact that it is the outpost of order and discipline.

In Jumburu were two brothers, O'ka and B'suru, who had usurped the chieftainship of their uncle, the very famous K'sungasa, "very famous," since he had been in his time a man of remarkable gifts, which he still retained to some extent, and in consequence enjoyed what was left of life.

He was, by all accounts, as mad as a man could be, and in circumstances less favourable to himself his concerned relatives would have taken him a long journey into the forest he loved so well, and they would have put out his eyes and left him to the mercy of the beasts, such being the method of dealing with lunacy amongst people who, all unknown to themselves, were eugenists of a most inflexible kind.

But to leave K'sungasa to the beasts would have been equivalent to delivering him to the care of his dearest friends, for he had an affinity for the wild dwellers of the bush, and all his life he had lived amongst them and loved them.

It is said that he could arrest the parrot in the air by a "cl'k!" and could bring the bird screeching and fluttering to his hand. He could call the shy little monkeys from the high branches where they hid, and even the fiercest of buffaloes would at his word come snuffling and nosing his brown arm.

So that, when he grew weak-minded, his relatives, after a long palaver, decided that for once the time-honoured customs of the land should be overridden, and since there was no other method of treating the blind but that prescribed by precedent, he should be allowed to live in a great hut at the edge of the village with his birds and snakes and wild-cats, and that the direction of village affairs should pass to his nephews.

Mr Commissioner Sanders knew all this, but did nothing. His task was to govern the territory, which meant to so direct affairs that the territory governed itself. When the fate of K'sungasa was in the balance, he sent word to the chief's nephews that he was somewhere in the neighbourhood, and that the revival of the bad old custom of blinding would be followed by the introduction of the bad new custom of hanging; but this had less effect upon the council of relatives – to whom Sanders' message was not transmitted – than the strangest friendship which K'sungasa had for the forest folk.

The nephews might have governed the village, exacted tribute, apportioned fishing rights, and administered justice for all time, but for the fact that there came a period of famine, when crops were bad and fish was scarce, and when, remarkably enough, the village of L'bini, distant no more than a few hours' paddling, had by a curious coincident raised record crops, and had, moreover a glut of fish in their waters.

There was the inevitable palaver and the inevitable solution. O'ka and B'suru led ten canoes to the offending village, slaughtered a few men and burnt a few huts. For two hours the combatants pranced and yelled and thrust at one another amidst a pandemonium of screaming women, and then Lieutenant Tibbetts dropped from the clouds with a most substantial platoon of Houssas, and there was a general sorting out.

Sanders held a court on one of the middle islands near the Residency, and B'suru was sent to the Village of Irons for the term of his natural life. O'ka, who had fled to the bush, escaped, however, and with him a headman and a few followers.

Lieutenant Tibbetts, who had spent two profitable days in the village of Jumburu, came back to the Residency a very thoughtful young man.

"What is the matter with Bones?" asked Captain Hamilton.

His sister smiled over her book, but offered no other comment.

"Do you know, Pat?" demanded Hamilton sternly.

Sanders looked at the girl with a twinkle in his grey eyes, and lit a cheroot. The relationships between Patricia Hamilton and Bones were a source of constant joy to him. Taciturn and a thought dour as he was, Pat would never have suspected the bubbling laughter which arose behind that lean brown face, unmovable and, in his moments of most intense enjoyment, expressionless.

"Bones and I have a feud," said the girl.

Sanders smiled.

"Not as violent a feud as O'ka and I have, I hope?" he said.

She frowned a little and looked at him anxiously.

"But you don't worry about the threats of the people you have punished?" she asked.

"I haven't punished O'ka," said Sanders, "and an expedition into the bush would be too expensive an affair. He has apparently settled with the B'wigini people. If they take up his feud, they might give trouble. But what is your trouble with Bones?"

"You must ask him," she said.

Hamilton's opportunity came next day, when Bones applied for leave.

"Leave?" said Captain Hamilton incredulously. "Leave, Bones? What the dickens do you want leave for?"

Bones, standing as stiff as a ramrod before the office table at which his superior sat, saluted.

"Urgent private affairs, sir," he said gruffly.

"But you haven't any private affairs," protested Hamilton. "Your life is an open book – you were bragging about that fact yesterday."

"Sir and brother-officer," said Bones firmly, "a crisis has arisen in my young life. My word, sir, has been called into doubt by your jolly old sister. I desire to vindicate my honour, my reputation, an' my veracity."

"Pat has been pulling your leg!" suggested Hamilton, but Bones shook his head.

"Nothin' so indelicate, sir. Your revered an' lovely relative – God bless her jolly old heart! – expressed her doubt in *re* leopards an' buffaloes. I'm goin' out, sir, into the wilds – amidst dangers, Ham, old feller, that only seasoned veterans like you an' me can imagine – to bring proof that I am not only a sportsman, but a gentleman."

The timely arrival of Miss Patricia Hamilton, very beautiful in dazzling white, with her solar helmet perched at an angle, smote Bones to silence.

"What have you been saying to Bones?" asked Hamilton severely.

"She said – "

"I said – "

They began and finished together.

"Bones, you're a tell-tale," accused the girl.

"Go on," said Bones recklessly. "Don't spare me. I'm a liar an' a thief an' a murderer – don't mind me!"

"I simply said that I didn't believe he shot the leopard – the one whose skin is in his hut."

"Oh, no," said Bones with heavy sarcasm, "I didn't shoot it – oh, no! I froze it to death – I poisoned it!"

"But did you shoot it?" she asked.

"Did I shoot it, dear old Ham?" asked Bones, with great calmness.

"Did you?" asked Hamilton innocently.

"Did I shoot at that leopard," Bones went on deliberately, "an' was he found next mornin' cold and dead, with a smile on his naughty old face?"

Hamilton nodded, and Bones faced the girl expectantly.

"Apologize, child," he said.

"I shall do nothing of the kind," she replied, with some heat. "Did Bones shoot the leopard?"

She appealed to her brother.

Hamilton looked from one to the other.

"When the leopard was found – " he began.

"Listen to this, dear old sister," murmured Bones.

"When the leopard was found, with a spear in its side – "

"Evidently done after death by a wanderin' cad of a native," interposed Bones hastily.

"Be quiet, Bones," commanded the girl, and Bones shrugged his shoulders and obeyed.

"When the leopard was found," continued Hamilton, "he was certainly beyond human aid, and though no bullet mark was discovered, Bones conclusively proved – "

"One moment, dear old officer," interrupted Bones. He had seen out of the tail of his eye a majestic figure crossing the square.

"Will you allow me to produce scientific an' expert evidence?"

Hamilton assented gravely, and Bones went to the door of the orderly room and roared a name.

"I shall produce," he said quietly, but firmly, "the evidence of one who enjoyed the confidence of dear old Professor What's-his-name, the eminent thingumy-ologist. Oh, Ali!"

Ali Abid, a solemn figure, salaamed in the doorway.

Not for nothing had he been factotum to a great bacteriologist before the demise of his master had driven him to service with a lieutenant of Houssas. His vocabulary smelt of the laboratory, his English was pure, undefiled, and unusual.

"Ali, you remember my leopard?"

"Sir," said Ali, shaking his head, "who can forget?"

"Did I kill him, Ali?" asked Bones. "Tell the lady everything."

Ali bowed to the girl.

"Miss or madame," he said, "the leopard (*Felis pardus*), a wild beast of the Felidae family, is indigenous to forest territory. The subject in question – to wit, the skin thereof exhibited by Sir Bones – was particularly ferocious, and departed this life as a result of hunting conducted by aforesaid. Examination of subject after demise under most scientific scrutiny revealed that said leopard (*Felis pardus*) suffered from weak heart, and primary cause of death was diagnosed as shock occasioned by large 'bang' from Sir Bones' rifle."

"What did I say?" asked Bones complacently.

"Do you mean to tell me," gasped the girl, "that you *frightened* the leopard to death?"

Bones spread out his hands disparagingly.

"You have heard the evidence, dear old sister," he said; "there is nothing to add."

She threw back her head and laughed until her grey eyes were swimming in tears.

"Oh, Bones, you humbug!" she laughed.

Bones drew himself up more stiffly than ever, stuck his monocle in his eye, and turned on his chief.

"Do I understand, sir," he said, "that my leave is granted?"

"Seven days," said Hamilton, and Bones swung round on his heel, knocked over Hamilton's stationery rack, stumbled over a chair, and strode gloomily from the hut.

When Patricia Hamilton woke the next morning, she found a note pinned to her pillow.

We may gloss over the impropriety of the proceedings which led to this phenomenon. Bones was an artist, and so small a matter as the proprieties did not come into his calculations.

Patricia sat up in bed and read the letter.

DEAR OLD FRIEND AND DOUTTING THOS.

(Bones' spelling was always perfectly disgraceful), –

When this reaches you, when this reaches you, I shall be far, far away on my long and dangerous journey. I may not come back, I may not come back, for I and a faithful servant are about to penetrate to the lares of the wild beasts of the forest, of the forest. I am determined to wipe out the reproach which you have made. I will bring back, not a dead leppard, not a dead leppard, but a live one, which I shall seeze with my own hands. I may lose my life in this rash and hazardus enterprise, but at least I shall vindycate my honour. – Farewell, dear old Patrisia.

Your friend,

B

"Which proves," said Hamilton, when he was shown the letter, "that Bones is learning to spell. It only seems yesterday when he was spelling 'Hamilton' with three m's. By the way, how did you get this letter?"

"I found it pinned to the door," said Patricia tactfully.

Bones went by the shortest route to Jumburu, and was received without enthusiasm, for he had left a new chief to rule over a people who were near enough to the B'wigini to resent overmuch discipline. But his business was with K'sungasa, for the two days' stay which Bones had made in the village, and all that he had learnt of the old tamer, had been responsible for his reckless promise to Patricia Hamilton.

He came at a critical moment, for K'sungasa, a thin and knobbly old man, with dim eyes and an incessant chuckle, was very near his end. He lay on a fine raised bed, a big yellow-eyed wild cat at his feet, a monkey or two shivering by the bedside, and a sprawling litter of kittens – to which the wild cat leapt in a tremble of rage when Bones entered the hut – crawling in the sunlight which flooded the hut.

"Lord Tibbetti," croaked the old man, "I see you! This is a good time, for tomorrow I should be dead."

"K'sungasa," said Bones, seating himself gingerly, and looking about for the snake which was usually coiled round the old man's stool, "that is foolish talk, for you will see many floods."

"That is fine talk for the river folk," grinned the old man, "but not for we people of the forest, who never see flood and only little-little rivers. Now, I tell you, lord, that I am glad to die, because I have been full of mad thoughts for a long time, but now my mind is clear. Tell me, master, why you come."

Bones explained his errand, and the old man's eyes brightened.

"Lord, if I could go with you to the forest, I would bring to you many beautiful leopards by my magic. Now, because I love Sandi, I will do this for you, so that you shall know how wise and cunning I am."

In the woods about the village was a wild plant, the seeds of which, when pounded and boiled in an earthern vessel, produced, by a rough method of distillation, a most pungent liquid. Abid spoke learnedly of *pimpinella anisum*, and probably he was right.*

Bones and his assistant made many excursions into the woods before they found and brought back the right plant. Fortunately it was seed-time, and once he was on the right track Bones had no difficulty in securing more than a sufficient quantity for his pupose.

He made his distillation under the old man's directions, the fire burning in the middle of the hut. As the drops began to fall from the narrow neck of his retort, a faint sweet aroma filled the hut. First the cat, then the monkeys began to show signs of extraordinary agitation. Cat and kittens crouched as near the fire as they could, their heads craned towards the brown vessel, mewing and whimpering. Then the monkeys came, bright-eyed and eager.

The scent brought the most unexpected beasts from every hole and crevice in the hut – brown rats, squirrels, a long black snake with spade-shaped head and diamond markings, little bush hares, a young buck, which came crashing through the forest and prinked timidly to the door of the hut.

* Both anise and star anise (*Illicium anisatum*) are to be found in the Territories, as also is a small plant which has all the properties (and more) of *Pimpinella anisum*. This was probably the plant. – AUTHOR.

The old man on the bed called them all by name, and snapped his feeble fingers to them; but their eyes were on the retort and the crystal drops that trembled and fell from the lip of the narrow spout.

A week later a speechless group stood before the Residency and focused their astonished gaze upon the miracle.

"The miracle" was a half-grown leopard cub, vividly marked. He was muzzled and held in leash by a chain affixed to a stout collar, and Bones, a picture of smug gratification, held the end of the chain.

"But how – how did you catch him?" gasped the girl.

Bones shrugged his shoulders.

"It is not for me, dear old friend, to tell of nights spent in the howlin' forest," he quavered, in the squeaky tone which invariably came to him when he was excited. "I'm not goin' to speak of myself. If you expect me to tell you how I trailed the jolly old leopard to his grisly lair an' fought with him single-handed, you'll be disappointed."

"But did you track him to his lair?" demanded Hamilton, recovering his speech.

"I beg of you, dear old officer, to discuss other matters," evaded Bones tactfully. "Here are the goods delivered, as per mine of the twenty-fourth instant."

He put his hand to his pocket mechanically, and the cub looked up with a quick eager stare.

"Bones, you're a wonderful fellow," said Sanders quietly.

Bones bowed.

"And now," he said, "if you'll excuse me, I'll take my little friend to his new home."

Before they realized what he was doing, he had slipped off the chain. Even Sanders stepped back and dropped his hand to the automatic pistol he carried in his hip pocket.

But Bones, unconcerned, whistled and marched off to his hut, and the great cat followed humbly at his heels.

That same night Bones strode across from his hut to the Residency, resolved upon a greater adventure yet. He would go out under the admiring eyes of Patricia Hamilton, and would return from the

Residency woods a veritable Pied Piper, followed by a trail of forest denizens.

In his pocket was a quart bottle, and his clothes reeked with the scent of wild aniseed. As a matter of fact, his secret would have been out the moment he entered Sanders' dining-room, but it so happened that his programme was doomed to interruption.

He was halfway across the square when a dark figure rose from the ground and a harsh voice grunted "Kill!"

He saw the flash of the spear in the starlight and leapt aside. A hand clutched at his jacket, but he wrenched himself free, leaving the garment in his assailant's hands.

He was unarmed, and there was nothing left but flight.

Sanders heard his yell, and sprang out to the darkness of the verandah as Bones flew up the steps.

He saw the two men racing in pursuit, and fired twice. One man fell, the other swerved and was lost in the shadows.

An answering shot came from the Houssa sentry at the far end of the square. Sanders saw a man running, and fired again, and again missed.

Then out of the darkness blundered Ali Abid, his face grey with fear.

"Sir, he gasped, "wild animal (*Felis pardus*) has divested muzzlement and proper restraint, and is chasing various subjects outrageously.".

Even as he spoke a fourth figure sped across the ground before the Residency, so close that they could see the bundle he carried under his arm.

"My jacket!" roared Bones. "Hi, stop him! Good Lord!"

Swift on the heels of the flying man came a streak of yellow fur…

Whether O'ka of the Jumburu outpaced the leopard, or the leopard overtook O'ka, is not known, but until the rains came and washed away the scent of crude aniseed, Bones dared not leave his hut by night for fear of the strange beasts that came snuffling at his hut, or sat in expectant and watchful circles about his dwelling, howling dismally.

# THE MERCENARIES

There was a large brown desk in Sanders' study, a desk the edges of which had been worn yellow with constant rubbing. It was a very tidy desk, with two rows of books neatly grouped on the left and on the right, and held in place by brass rails. There were three tiers of wire baskets, a great white blotting-pad, a silver inkstand and four clean-looking pens.

Lately, there had appeared a glass vase filled with flowers which were daily renewed. Except on certain solemn occasions, none intruded into this holy of holies. It is true that a change had been brought about by the arrival of Patricia Hamilton, for she had been accorded permission to use the study as she wished, and she it was who had introduced the floral decorations.

Yet, such was the tradition of sanctuary which enveloped the study, that neither Captain Hamilton, her brother, nor Bones, her slave, had ever ventured to intrude thither in search of her, and if by chance they came to the door to speak to her, they unaccountably lowered their voices.

On a certain summer morning, Hamilton sat at the desk, a stern and sober figure, and Bones, perspiring and rattled, sat on the edge of a chair facing him.

The occasion was a solemn one, for Bones was undergoing his examination in subjects "X" and "Y" for promotion to the rank of Captain. The particular subject under discussion was "Map Reading and Field Sketching," and the inquisition was an oral one.

113

"Lieutenant Tibbetts," said Hamilton gravely, "you will please define a Base Line."

Bones pushed back the hair straggling over his forehead, and blinked rapidly in an effort of memory.

"A base line, dear old officer?" he repeated. "A base line, dear old Ham – "

"Restrain your endearing terms," said Hamilton, "you won't get any extra marks for 'em."

"A base line?" mused Bones; then, "Whoop! I've got it! God bless your jolly old soul! I thought I'd foozled it. A base line," he said loudly, "is the difference of level between two adjacent contours. How's that, umpire?"

"Wrong," said Hamilton; "you're describing a Vertical Interval."

Bones glared at him.

"Are you sure, dear old chap?" he demanded truculently. "Have a look at the book, jolly old friend, your poor old eyes ain't what they used to be – "

"Lieutenant Tibbetts," said Hamilton in ponderous reproof, "you are behaving very strangely."

"Look here, dear old Ham," wheedled Bones, "can't you pretend you asked me what a Vertical Interval was?"

Hamilton reached round to find something to throw, but this was Sanders' study.

"You have a criminal mind, Bones," he said helplessly.

"Now get on with it. What are' Hachures'?"

"Hachures?" said Bones, shutting his eye. "Hachures? Now I know what Hachures are. A lot of people would think they were chickens, but I know…they're a sort of line…when you're drawing a hill… wiggly-waggly lines…you know the funny things…a sort of…" Bones made mysterious and erratic gestures in the air, "shading… water, dear old friend."

"Are you feeling faint?" asked Hamilton, jumping up in alarm.

"No, silly ass…shadings…direction of water – am I right sir?"

"Not being a thought-reader I can't visualize your disordered mind," said Hamilton, "but Hachures are the conventional method of representing hill features by shading in short vertical lines to indicate the slope and the water flow. I gather that you have a hazy idea of what the answer should be."

"I thank you, dear old sir, for that generous tribute to my grasp of military science," said Bones. "An' now proceed to the next torture — which will you have, sir, rack or thumbscrew? — oh, thank you, Horace, I'll have a glass of boiling oil."

"Shut up talking to yourself," growled Hamilton, "and tell me what is meant by 'Orienting a Map'?"

"Turning it to the east," said Bones promptly. "Next sir."

"What is meant by 'Orienting a Map'?" asked Hamilton patiently.

"I've told you once," said Bones defiantly.

"Orienting a Map," said Hamilton, "as I have explained to you a thousand times, means setting your map or planetable so that the north line lies north."

"In that case, sir," replied Bones firmly, "the east line would be east, and I claim to have answered the question to your entire satisfaction."

"Continue to claim," snarled Hamilton. "I shall mark you zero for that answer."

"Make it one," pleaded Bones. "Be a sport, dear old Ham — I've found a new fishin' pool."

Hamilton hesitated.

"There are never any fish in the pools you find," he said dubiously. "Anyway, I'll reserve my decision until I've made a cast or two."

They adjourned for tiffin soon after.

"How did you do, Bones?" asked Patricia Hamilton.

"Fine," said Bones enthusiastically; "I simply bowled over every question that your dear old brother asked. In fact, Ham admitted that I knew much more about some things than he did."

"What I said," corrected Hamilton, "was that your information on certain subjects was so novel that I doubted whether even the staff college shared it."

"It's the same thing," said Bones.

"You should try him on military history," suggested Sanders dryly. "I've just been hearing from Bosambo — "

Bones coughed and blushed.

"The fact is, sir an' Excellency," he confessed, "I was practisin' on Bosambo. You mightn't be aware of the fact, but I like to hear myself speak – "

"No!" gasped Hamilton in amazement, "you're wronging yourself, Bones!"

"What I mean, sir," Bones went on with dignity, "is that if I lecture somebody on a subject I remember what I've said."

"Always providing that you understand what you're saying," suggested Hamilton.

"Anyway," said Sanders, with his quiet smile, "Bones has filled Bosambo with a passionate desire to emulate Napoleon, and Bosambo has been making tentative inquiries as to whether he can raise an Old Guard or enlist a mercenary army."

"I flatter myself – " began Bones.

"Why not?" said Hamilton, rising. "It's the only chance you'll have of hearing something complimentary about yourself."

"*I* believe in you, Bones," said a smiling Patricia. "I think you're really wonderful, and that Ham is a brute."

"I'll never, never contradict you, dear Miss Patricia," said Bones; "an' after the jolly old Commissioner has gone – "

"You're not going away again, are you?" she asked, turning to Sanders. "Why, you have only just come back from the interior."

There was genuine disappointment in her eyes, and Sanders experienced a strange thrill the like of which he had never known before.

"Yes," he said with a nod. "There is a palaver of sorts in the Morjaba country – the most curious palaver I have ever been called upon to hold."

And indeed he spoke the truth.

Beyond the frontiers of the Akasava, and separated from all the other Territories by a curious bush belt which ran almost in a straight line for seventy miles, were the people of Morjaba. They were a folk isolated from territorial life, and Sanders saw them once every year and no more frequently, for they were difficult to come by, regular payers of taxes and law–abiding, having quarrels with none. The bush (reputedly the abode of ghosts) was, save at one point, impenetrable. Nature had plaited a natural wall on one side, and had given the tribe the protection of high mountains to the north and a broad swamp to the west.

The fierce storms of passion and hate which burst upon the river at intervals and sent thousands of spears to a blooding, were scarcely echoed in this sanctuary-land. The marauders of the Great King's country to the north never fetched across the smooth moraine of the mountains, and the evil people of The-Land-beyond-the-Swamp were held back by the treacherous bog-land wherein, *cala-cala*, a whole army had been swallowed up.

Thus protected, the Morjabian folk grew fat and rich. The land was a veritable treasure of Nature, and it is a fact that in the dialect they speak, there is no word which means "hunger."*

Yet the people of the Morjaba were not without their crises.

S'kobi, the stout chief, held a great court which was attended by ten thousand people, for at that court was to be concluded for ever the feud between the M'gimi and the M'joro – a feud which went back for the greater part of fifty years.

The M'gimi were the traditional warrior tribe, the bearers of arms, and, as their name ("The High Lookers") implied, the proudest and most exclusive of the people. For every man was the descendant of a chief, and it was "easier for fish to walk," as the saying goes, than for a man of the M'joro ("The Diggers") to secure admission to the caste. Three lateral cuts on either cheek was the mark of the M'gimi – wounds made, upon the warrior's initiation to the order, with the razor-edged blade of a killing-spear. They lived apart in three camps to the number of six thousand men, and for five years from the hour of their initiation they neither married nor courted. The M'gimi turned their backs to women, and did not suffer their presence in their camps. And if any man departed from this austere rule he was taken

---

* It is as curious a fact that amongst the majority of cannibal people there is no equivalent for "thank you." – E W.

to the Breaking Tree, his four limbs were fractured, and he was hoisted to the lower branches, between which a litter was swung, and his regiment sat beneath the tree neither eating, drinking nor sleeping until he died. Sometimes this was a matter of days. As for the woman who had tempted his eye and his tongue, she was a witness.

Thus the M'gimi preserved their traditions of austerity. They were famous walkers and jumpers. They threw heavy spears and fought great sham-fights, and they did every violent exercise save till the ground.

This was the sum and substance of the complaint which had at last come to a head.

S'gono, the spokesman of The Diggers, was a headman of the inner lands, and spoke with bitter prejudice, since his own son had been rejected by the M'gimi captains as being unworthy.

"Shall we men dig and sow for such as these?" he asked. "Now give a judgment, King! Every moon we must take the best of our fruit and the finest of our fish. Also so many goats and so much salt, and it is swallowed up."

"Yet if I send them away," said the king, "how shall I protect this land against the warriors of the Akasava and the evil men of the swamp? Also of the Ochori, who are four days' march across good ground?"

"Lord King," said S'gono, "are there no M'gimi amongst us who have passed from the camp and have their women and their children? May not these take the spear again? And are not we M'joro folk men? By my life! I will raise as many spears from The Diggers and captain them with M'joro men – this I could do between the moons and none would say that you were not protected. For we are men as bold as they."

The king saw that the M'gimi party were in the minority. Moreover, he had little sympathy with the warrior caste, for his beginnings were basely rooted in the soil, and two of his sons had no more than scraped into the M'gimi.

"This thing shall be done," said the king, and the roar of approval which swept up the little hillock on which he sat was his reward.

Sanders, learning something of these doings, had come in haste, moving across the Lower Akasava by a short cut, risking the chagrin of certain chiefs and friends who would be shocked and mortified by his apparent lack of courtesy in missing the ceremonious call which was their due.

But his business was very urgent otherwise he would not have travelled by Nobolama – The River-that-comes-and goes.

He was fortunate in that he found deep water for the *Wiggle* as far as the edge of this pleasant land. A two days' trek through the forest brought him to the great city of Morjaba. In all the Territories there was no such city as this, for it stretched for miles on either hand, and indeed was one of the most densely populated towns within a radius of five hundred miles.

S'kobi came waddling to meet his governor with maize, plucked in haste from the gardens he passed, and salt, grabbed at the first news of Sanders' arrival, in his big hands. These he extended as he puffed to where Sanders sat at the edge of the city.

"Lord," he wheezed, "none came with news of this great honour, or my young men would have met you, and my maidens would have danced the road flat with their feet. Take!"

Sanders extended both palms and received the tribute of salt and corn, and solemnly handed the crushed mess to his orderly.

"O S'kobi," he said, "I came swiftly to make a secret palaver with you, and my time is short."

"Lord, I am your man," said S'kobi, and signalled his councillors and elder men to a distance.

Sanders was in some difficulty to find a beginning.

"You know, S'kobi, that I love your people as my children," he said, "for they are good folk who are faithful to government and do ill to none."

"Wa!" said S'kobi.

"Also you know that spearmen and warriors I do not love, for spears are war and warriors are great lovers of fighting."

"Lord, you speak the truth," said the other, nodding, "therefore in this land I will have made a law that there shall be no spears, save those which sleep in the shadow of my hut. Now well I know why you have come to make this palaver, for you have heard with your beautiful long ears that I have sent away my fighting regiments."

Sanders nodded.

"You speak truly, my friend," he said, and S'kobi beamed.

"Six times a thousand spears I had – and, lord spears grow no corn. Rather are they terrible eaters. And now I have sent them to their villages, and at the next moon they should have burnt their fine war-knives, but for a certain happening. We folk of Morjaba have no enemies, and we do good to all. Moreover, lord, as you know, we have amongst us many folk of the Isisi, of the Akasava and the N'gombi, also men from the Great King's land beyond the High Rocks, and the little folk from The-Land-beyond-the-Swamp. Therefore, who shall attack us since we have kinsmen of all amongst us?"

Sanders regarded the jovial king with a sad little smile.

"Have I done well by all men?" he asked quietly. "Have I not governed the land so that punishment comes swiftly to those who break the law? Yet, S'kobi, do not the Akasava and the Isisi, the N'gombi and the Lower River folk take their spears against me? Now I tell you this which I have discovered. In all beasts great and little there are mothers who have young ones and fathers who fight that none shall harass the mother."

"Lord, this is the way of life," said S'kobi.

"It is the way of the Bigger Life," said Sanders, "and greatly the way of man-life. For the women bring children to the land and the men sit with their spears ready to fight all who would injure their women. And so long as life lasts, S'kobi, the women will bear and the men will guard; it is the way of Nature, and you shall not take from men the desire for slaughter until you have dried from the hearts of women the yearning for children."

"Lord," said S'kobi, a fat man and easily puzzled, "what shall be the answer to this strange riddle you set me?"

"Only this," said Sanders rising, "I wish peace in this land, but there can be no peace between the leopard who has teeth and claws and the rabbit who has neither tooth nor claw. Does the leopard fight the lion or the lion the leopard? They live in peace, for each is terrible in his way, and each fears the other. I tell you this, that you live in love with your neighbours not because of your kindness, but because of your spears. Call them back to your city, S'kobi."

The chief's large face wrinkled in a frown.

"Lord," he said, "that cannot be, for these men have marched away from my country to find a people who will feed them, for they are too proud to dig the ground."

"Oh, damn!" said Sanders in despair, and went back the way he came, feeling singularly helpless.

The Odyssey of the discarded army of the Morjaba has yet to be written. Paradoxically enough, its primary mission was a peaceful one, and when it found first the frontiers of the Akasava and then the river borders of the Isis closed against it, it turned to the north in an endeavour to find service under the Great King, beyond the mountains. Here it was repulsed and its pacific intentions scouted. The M'gimi formed a camp a day's march from the Ochori border, and were on the thin line which separates unemployment from anarchy when Bosambo, Chief of the Ochori, who had learnt of their presence, came upon the scene.

Bosambo was a born politician. He had the sense of opportunity and that strange haze of hopeful but indefinite purpose which is the foundation of the successful poet and statesman, but which, when unsuccessfully developed, is described as "temperament."

Bones, paying a business call upon the Ochori, found a new township grown up on the forest side of the city. He also discovered evidence of discontent in Bosambo's harassed people, who had been called upon to provide fish and meal for the greater part of six thousand men who were too proud to work.

"Master," said Bosambo, "I have often desired such an army as this, for my Ochori fighters are few. Now, lord, with these men I can hold the Upper River for your King and Sandi, and none dare speak against him. Thus would N'poloyani, who is your good friend, have done."

"But who shall feed these men, Bosambo?" demanded Bones hastily.

"All things are with God," replied Bosambo piously.

Bones collected all the available information upon the matter and took it back to headquarters.

"H'm," said Sanders when he had concluded his recital, "if it had been any other man but Bosambo…you would require another battalion, Hamilton."

"But what has Bosambo done?" asked Patricia Hamilton, admitted to the council.

"He is being Napoleonic," said Sanders, with a glance at the youthful authority on military history, and Bones squirmed and made strange noises. "We will see how it works out. How on earth is he going to feed them, Bones?"

"Exactly the question I asked, sir an' Excellency," said Bones in triumph. " 'Why, you silly old ass – ' "

"I beg your pardon!" exclaimed the startled Sanders.

"That is what I said to Bosambo, sir," explained Bones hastily. " 'Why, you silly old ass,' I said, 'how are you goin' to grub 'em?' 'Lord Bones,' said Bosambo, 'that's the jolly old problem that I'm workin' out.' "

How Bosambo worked out his problem may be gathered.

"There is some talk of an Akasava rising," said Sanders at breakfast one morning. "I don't know why this should be, for my information is that the Akasava folk are fairly placid."

"Where does the news come from, sir?" asked Hamilton.

"From the Isisi king – he's in a devil of a funk, and has begged Bosambo to send him help."

That help was forthcoming in the shape of Bosambo's new army, which arrived on the outskirts of the Isisi city and sat in idleness for a month, at the end of which time the people of the Isisi represented to their king that they would, on the whole, prefer war to a peace which put them on half rations in order that six thousand proud warriors might live on the fat of the land.

The M'gimi warriors marched back to the Ochori, each man carrying a month's supply of maize and salt, wrung from the resentful peasants of the Isisi.

Three weeks after, Bosambo sent an envoy to the King of the Akasava.

"Let no man know this, Gubara, lest it come to the ears of Sandi, and you, who are very innocent, be wrongly blamed," said the envoy solemnly. "This says Bosambo: It has come to my ears that the N'gombi are secretly arming and will very soon send a forest of spears against the Akasava. Say this to Gubara, that because my stomach is filled with sorrow I will help him. Because I am very powerful, because of my friendship with Bonesi and his cousin, N'poloyani, who is also married to Bonesi's aunt, I have a great army which I will send to the Akasava, and when the N'gombi hear of this they will send away their spears and there will be peace."

The Akasava chief, a nervous man with the memory of all the discomforts which follow tribal wars, eagerly assented. For two months Bosambo's army sat down like a cloud of locusts and ate the Akasava to a condition bordering upon famine.

At the end of that time they marched to the N'gombi country, news having been brought by Bosambo's messengers that the Great King was crossing the western mountains with a terrible army to seize the N'gombi forests. How long this novel method of provisioning his army might have continued may only be guessed, for in the midst of Bosambo's plans for maintaining an army at the expense of his neighbours there was a great happening in the Morjaba country.

S'kobi, the fat chief, had watched the departure of his warriors with something like relief. He was gratified, moreover (native-like), by the fact that he had confounded Sanders. But when the Commissioner had gone and S'kobi remembered all that he had said, a great doubt settled like a pall upon his mind. For three days he sat, a dejected figure, on the high carved stool of state before his house, and at the end of that time he summoned S'gono, the M'joro.

"S'gono," said he, "I am troubled in my stomach because of certain things which our lord Sandi has said."

Thereupon he told the plebeian councillor much of what Sanders had said.

"And now my M'gimi are with Bosambo of the Ochori, and he sells them to this people and that for so much treasure and food."

"Lord," said S'gono, "is my word nothing? Did I not say that I would raise spears more wonderful than the M'gimi? Give me leave, King, and you shall find an army that shall grow in a night. I, S'gono, son of Mocharlabili Yoka, say this!"

So messengers went forth to all the villages of the Morjaba calling the young men to the King's hut, and on the third week there stood on a plateau beneath the king's palaver house a most wonderful host.

"Let them march across the plain and make the Dance of Killing," said the satisfied king, and S'gono hesitated.

"Lord King," he pleaded, "these are new soldiers, and they are not yet wise in the ways of warriors. Also they will not take the chiefs I gave them, but have chosen their own, so that each company have two leaders who say evil things of one another."

S'kobi opened his round eyes.

"The M'gimi did not do this," he said dubiously, "for when their captains spoke they leapt first with one leg and then with the other, which was beautiful to see and very terrifying to our enemies."

"Lord," begged the agitated S'gono, "give me the space of a moon and they shall leap with both legs and dance in a most curious manner."

A spy retailed this promise to a certain giant chief of the Great King who was sitting on the Morjaba slopes of the mountains with four thousand spears, awaiting a favourable moment to ford the river which separated him from the rich lands of the northern Morjaba.

This giant heard the tidings with interest.

"Soon they shall leap without heads," he said, "for without the M'gimi they are little children. For twenty seasons we have waited, and now comes our fine night. Go you, B'furo, to the Chief of The-Folk-beyond-the-Swamp and tell him that when he sees three fires on this mountain he shall attack across the swamp by the road which he knows."

It was a well-planned campaign which the Great King's generals and the Chief of The-People-beyond-the-Marsh had organized. With the passing of the warrior caste the enemies of the Morjaba had moved swiftly. The path across the swamp had been known for years, but the M'gimi had had one of their camps so situated that no enemy could debouch across, and had so ordered their dispositions that the northern river boundary was automatically safeguarded.

Now S'gono was a man of the fields, a grower and seller of maize and a breeder of goats. And he had planned his new army as he would plan a new garden, on the basis that the nearer the army was to the capital, the easier it was to maintain. In consequence the river-ford was unguarded, and there were two thousand spears across the marshes before a scared minister of war apprehended any danger.

He flung his new troops against the Great King's chief captain in a desperate attempt to hold back the principal invader. At the same time, more by luck than good generalship, he pushed the evil people of the marsh back to their native element.

For two days the Morjaba fought desperately if unskilfully against the seasoned troops of the Great King, while messengers hurried east and south, seeking help.

Bosambo's intelligence department may have shown remarkable prescience in unearthing the plot against the peace and security of the Morjaba, or it may have been (and this is Sanders' theory) that Bosambo was on his way to the Morjaba with a cock and bull story of imminent danger. He was on the frontier when the king's messenger came, and Bosambo returned with the courier to treat in person.

"Five thousand loads of corn I will give you, Bosambo," said the king, "also a hundred bags of salt. Also two hundred women who shall be slaves in your house."

There was some bargaining, for Bosambo had no need of slaves, but urgently wanted goats. In the end he brought up his hirelings, and the people of the Morjaba city literally fell on the necks of the returned M'gimi.

The enemy had forced the northern defences and were half-way to the city when the M'gimi fell upon their flank.

The giant chief of the Great King's army saw the ordered ranks of the old army driving in his flank, and sent for his own captain.

"Go swiftly to our lord, the King, and say that I am a dead man."

He spoke no more than the truth, for he fell at the hand of Bosambo, who made a mental resolve to increase his demand on the herds of S'kobi in consequence.

For the greater part of a month Bosambo was a welcome visitor, and at the end of that time he made his preparations to depart.

Carriers and herdsmen drove or portered his reward back to the Ochori country, marching one day ahead of the main body.

The M'gimi were summoned for the march at dawn, but at dawn Bosambo found himself alone on the plateau, save for the few Ochori headmen who had accompanied him on his journey.

"Lord," said S'kobi, "my fine soldiers do not go with you, for I have seen how wise is Sandi who is my father and my mother."

Bosambo choked, and as was usual in moments of intense emotion, found refuge in English.

"Dam' nigger!" he said wrathfully, "I bring um army, I feed um, I keep um proper – you pinch um! Black t'ief! Pig! You bad feller! I speak you bad for N'poloyani – him fine feller."

"Lord," said the uncomprehending king, "I see that you are like Sandi for you speak his tongue. He also said 'Dam' very loudly. I think it is the word white folk say when they are happy."

Bosambo met Bones hurrying to the scene of the fighting, and told his tale.

"Lord," he said in conclusion, "what was I to do, for you told nothing of the ways of N'poloyani when his army was stolen from him. Tell me now, Tibbetti, what this man would have done."

But Bones shook his head severely.

"This I cannot tell you, Bosambo," he said, "for if I do you will tell others, and my lord N'poloyani will never forgive me."

# THE WATERS OF MADNESS

Unexpected things happen in the Territories which Mr Commissioner Sanders rules. As for example: Bones had gone down to the beach to "take the mail." This usually meant no more than receiving a mail-bag wildly flung from a dancing surf-boat. On this occasion Bones was surprised to discover that the boat had beached and had landed, not only the mail, but a stranger with his baggage.

He was a clean-shaven, plump man, in spotless white, and he greeted Bones with a friendly nod. "Morning!" he said. "I've got your mail."

Bones extended his hand and took the bag without evidence of any particular enthusiasm.

"Sanders about?" asked the stranger.

"Mr Sanders is in residence, sir," said Bones, ponderously polite.

The other laughed. "Show the way," he said briskly.

Bones looked at the new-comer from the ventilator of his pith helmet to the soles of his pipe-clayed shoes. "Excuse me, dear old sir," he said, "have I the honour of addressin' the Secretary of State for War?"

"No," answered the other in surprise. "What made you think that?"

"Because," said Bones, with rising wrath, "he's the only fellow that needn't say 'please' to me."

The man roared with laughter. "Sorry," he said. "*Please* show me the way."

"Follow me, sir," said Bones.

Sanders was not "in residence," being, in fact, inspecting some recent – and native – repairs to the boilers of the *Zaire*.

The stranger drew up a chair on the stoep without invitation and seated himself. He looked around. Patricia Hamilton was at the far end of the stoep, reading a book. She had glanced up just long enough to note and wonder at the new arrival. "Deuced pretty girl that," said the stranger, lighting a cigar.

"I beg your pardon?" said Bones.

"I say that is a deuced pretty girl," said the stranger.

"And you're a deuced brute, dear sir," said Bones, "but hitherto I have not commented on the fact."

The man looked up quickly. "What are you here," he asked – "a clerk or something?"

Bones did not so much as flush. "Oh, no," he said sweetly. "I am an officer of Houssas – rank, lieutenant. My task is to tame the uncivilized beast an' entertain the civilized pig with a selection of music. Would you like to hear our gramophone?"

The new-comer frowned. What brilliant effort of persiflage was to follow will never be known, for at that moment came Sanders.

The stranger rose and produced a pocket-book, from which he extracted a card and a letter. "Good morning, Commissioner!" he said. "My name's Corklan – P T Corklan of Corklan, Besset and Lyons."

"Indeed," said Sanders.

"I've got a letter for you," said the man.

Sanders took the note, opened it, and read. It bore the neat signature of an Under-Secretary of State and the embossed heading of the Extra-Territorial Office, and it commended Mr P T Corklan to Mr Commissioner Sanders, and requested him to let Mr Corklan pass without let or hindrance through the Territories, and to render him every assistance "compatible with exigencies of the Service" in his "inquiries into sugar production from the sweet potato."

"You should have taken this to the Administrator," said Sanders, "and it should bear his signature."

"There's the letter," said the man shortly. "If that's not enough, and the signature of the Secretary of State isn't sufficient, I'm going straight back to England to tell him so."

"You may go to the devil and tell him so," said Sanders calmly; "but you do not pass into these Territories until I have received telegraphic authority from my chief. Bones, take this man to your hut, and let your people do what they can for him." And he turned and walked into the house.

"You shall hear about this," said Mr Corklan, picking up his baggage.

"This way, dear old pilgrim," said Bones.

"Who's going to carry my bag?"

"Your name escapes me," said Bones, "but, if you'll glance at your visitin' card, you will find the name of the porter legibly inscribed."

Sanders compressed the circumstances into a hundred-word telegram worded in his own economical style.

It happened that the Administrator was away on a shooting trip, and it was his cautious secretary who replied – "Administration to Sanders. – Duplicate authority here. Let Corklan proceed at own risk. Warn him dangers."

"You had better go along and tell him," said Sanders. "He can leave at once, and the sooner the better."

Bones delivered the message. The man was sitting on his host's bed, and the floor was covered with cigar ash. Worst abomination of all, was a large bottle of whisky, which he had produced from one of his bags, and a reeking glass, which he had produced from Bones' sideboard.

"So I can go tonight, can I?" said Mr Corklan. "That's all right. Now, what about conveyance, hey?"

Bones had now reached the stage where he had ceased to be annoyed, and when he found some interest in the situation.

"What sort of conveyance would you like, sir?" he asked curiously.

(If you can imagine him pausing half a bar before every "sir," you may value its emphasis.)

"Isn't there a steamer I can have?" demanded the man. "Hasn't Sanders got a Government steamer?"

"Pardon my swooning," said Bones, sinking into a chair.

"Well, how am I going to get up?" asked the man.

"Are you a good swimmer?" demanded Bones innocently.

"Look here," said Mr Corklan, "you aren't a bad fellow. I rather like you."

"I'm sorry," said Bones simply.

"I rather like you," repeated Mr Corklan. "You might give me a little help."

"It is very unlikely that I shall," said Bones. "But produce your proposition, dear old adventurer."

"That is just what I am," said the other. He bit off the end of another cigar and lit it with the glowing butt of the old one. "I have knocked about all over the world, and I have done everything. I've now a chance of making a fortune. There is a tribe here called the N'gombi. They live in a wonderful rubber country, and I am told that they have got all the ivory in the world, and stacks of rubber hidden away."

Now, it is a fact, – and Bones was surprised to hear it related by the stranger – that the N'gombi are great misers and hoarders of elephant tusks. For hundreds of years they have traded ivory and rubber, and every village has its secret storehouse. The Government had tried for years to wheedle the N'gombi into depositing their wealth in some State store, for riches mean war sooner or later. They lived in great forests – the word N'gombi means "interior" – in lands full of elephants and rich in rubber trees.

"You are a regular information bureau," said Bones admiringly. "But what has this to do with your inquiry into the origin of the candy tree?"

The man smoked in silence for a while, then he pulled from his pocket a big map. Again Bones was surprised, because the map he produced was the official map of the Territories. He traced the river with his fat forefinger.

"Here is the N'gombi country from the east bank of the Isisi, and this is all forest, and a rubber tree to every ten square yards."

"I haven't counted them," said Bones, "but I'll take your word."

"Now, what does this mean?" Mr Corklan indicated a twisting line of dots and dashes which began at the junction of the Isisi River and the Great River, and wound tortuously over five hundred miles of country until it struck the Sigi River, which runs through Spanish territory. "What is that?" he asked.

"That, or those," said Bones, "are the footprints of the mighty swoozlum bird that barks with its eyes an' lives on buttered toast an' hardware."

"I will tell you what I know it is," said the man, looking up and looking Bones straight in the eye – "it is one of those secret rivers you are always finding in these 'wet' countries. The natives tell you about 'em, but you never find 'em. They are rivers that only exist about once in a blue moon, when the river is very high and the rains are very heavy. Now, down in the Spanish territory" – he touched Bones' knees with great emphasis – "they tell me that their end of the secret river is in flood."

"They will tell you anything in the Spanish territory," said Bones pleasantly. "They'd tell you your jolly old fortune if you'd cross their palms with silver."

"What about your end?" asked the man, ignoring the scepticism of his host.

"Our end?" said Bones. "Well, you will find out for yourself. I'd hate to disappoint you."

"Now how am I going up?" asked the man, after a pause.

"You can hire a canoe, and live on the land, unless you have brought stores."

The man chuckled. "I've brought no stores. Here, I will show you something," he said. "You are a very good fellow." He opened his bag and took out a tight packet which looked like thin skins. There must have been two or three hundred of them. "That's my speciality," he said. He nipped the string that tied them together, stripped one off,

131

and, putting his lips to one end, blew. The skin swelled up like a toy balloon. "Do you know what that is?"

"No, I cannot say I do," said Bones.

"You have heard of Soemmering's process?"

Bones shook his head.

"Do you know what decimal 1986 signifies?"

"You've got me guessing, my lad," said Bones admiringly. The other chuckled, threw the skins into his bag, and closed it with a snap. "That's my little joke," he said. "All my friends tell me it will be the death of me one of these days. I like to puzzle people" – he smiled amiably and triumphantly in Bones' face – "I like to tell them the truth in such a way they don't understand it. If they understood it – Heavens there'd be the devil to pay!"

"You are an ingenious fellow," said Bones, "but I don't like your face. You will forgive my frankness, dear old friend."

"Faces aren't fortunes," said the other complacently, "and I am going out of this country with money sticking to me."

"I'm sorry for you," said Bones, shaking his head; "I hate to see fellows with illusions."

He reported all that occurred to the Commissioner, and Sanders was a little worried.

"I wish I knew what his game is," he said; "I'd stop him like a shot, but I can't very well in the face of the Administrator's wire. Anyway, he will get nothing out of the N'gombi. I've tried every method to make the beggars bank their surpluses, and I have failed."

"He has got to come back this way, at any rate," said Hamilton, "and I cannot see that he will do much harm."

"What is the rest of his baggage like?"

"He has a case of things that look like concave copper plates, sir," said Bones, "very thin copper, but copper. Then he has two or three copper pipes, and that is about his outfit."

Mr Corklan was evidently no stranger to the coast, and Bones, who watched the man's canoe being loaded that afternoon, and heard his fluent observations on the slackness of his paddlers, realized that his acquaintance with Central Africa was an extensive one. He cursed in Swahili and Portuguese, and his language was forcible and impolite. "Well," he said at last, "I'll be getting along. I'll make a fishing village for the night, and I ought to reach my destination in a week. I shan't be seeing you again, so I'll say goodbye."

"How do you suppose you're going to get out of the country?" asked Bones curiously.

Mr Corklan laughed. "So long!" he said.

"One moment, my dashin' old explorer," said Bones. "A little formality – I want to see your trunks opened."

A look of suspicion dawned on the man's face. "What for?"

"A little formality, my jolly old hero," said Bones.

"Why didn't you say so before?" growled the man, and had his two trunks landed. "I suppose you know you're exceeding your duty?"

"I didn't know – thanks for tellin' me," said Bones. "The fact is, sir an' fellow-man, I'm the Custom House officer."

The man opened his bags, and Bones explored. He found three bottles of whisky, and these he extracted.

"What's the idea?" asked Mr Corklan.

Bones answered him by breaking the bottles on a near-by stone.

"Here, what the dicken—"

"Wine is a mocker," said Bones, "strong drink is ragin'. This is what is termed in the land of Hope an' Glory a prohibition State, an' I'm entitled to fine you five hundred of the brightest an' best for attemptin' to smuggle intoxicants into our innocent country."

Bones expected an outburst; instead, his speech evoked no more than a snigger.

"You're funny," said the man.

"My friends tell me so," admitted Bones. "But there's nothin' funny about drink. Acquainted as you are with the peculiar workin's of the native psychology, dear sir, you will understand the primitive cravin' of the untutored mind for the enemy that we put in our mouths to steal away our silly old brains. I wish you 'bon voyage'."

"So long," said Mr Corklan.

Bones went back to the Residency and made his report, and there, for the time being, the matter ended. It was not unusual for wandering scientists, manufacturers, and representatives of shipping companies to arrive armed with letters of introduction or command, and to be dispatched into the interior. These visits, happily, were few and far between. On this occasion Sanders, being uneasy, sent one of his spies to follow the adventurer, with orders to report any extraordinary happening – a necessary step to take, for the N'gombi, and especially the Inner N'gombi, are a secretive people, and news from local sources is hard to come by.

"I shall never be surprised to learn that a war has been going on in the N'gombi for two months without our hearing a word about it."

"If they fight amongst themselves – yes," said Captain Hamilton; "if they fight outsiders, there will be plenty of bleats. Why not send Bones to overlook his sugar experiments," he added.

"Let's talk about something pleasant," said Bones hastily.

It was exactly three months later when he actually made the trip.

"Take the *Zaire* up to the bend of the Isisi," said Sanders one morning, at breakfast, "and find out what Ali Kano is doing – the lazy beggar should have reported."

"Any news from the N'gombi?" asked Hamilton.

"Only roundabout stories of their industry. Apparently the sugar merchant is making big experiments. He has set half the people digging roots for him. Be ready to sail at dawn."

"Will it be a dangerous trip?" asked the girl.

"No. Why?" smiled Sanders.

"Because I'd like to go. Oh, please, don't look so glum! Bones is awfully good to me."

"Better than a jolly old brother," murmured Bones.

"H'm!" Sanders shook his head, and she appealed to her brother. "Please!"

"I wouldn't mind your going," said Hamilton, "if only to look after Bones."

"S–sh!" said Bones reproachfully.

"If you're keen on it, I don't see why you shouldn't – if you had a chaperon."

"A chaperon!" sneered Bones. "Great Heavens! Do, old skipper, pull yourself together. Open the jolly old window and give him air. Feelin' better, sir?"

"A chaperon! How absurd!" cried the girl indignantly. "I'm old enough to be Bones' mother! I'm nearly twenty – well, I'm older than Bones, and I'm ever so much more capable of looking after myself."

The end of it was that she went, with her Kano maid and with the wife of Abiboo to cook for her. And in two days they came to the bend of the river, and Bones pursued his inquiries for the missing spy, but without success.

"But this I tell you, lord," said the little chief who acted as Sanders' agent, "that there are strange things happening in the N'gombi country, for all the people have gone mad, and are digging up their teeth (tusks) and bringing them to a white man."

"This shall go to Sandi," said Bones, realizing the importance of the news; and that same evening he turned the bow of the *Zaire* down stream.

Thus said Wafa, the half-breed, for he was neither foreign Arab nor native N'gombi, yet combined the cunning of both – "Soon we shall see the puc-a-puc of Government turn from the crookedness of the river, and I will go out and speak to our lord Tibbetti, who is a very simple man, and like a child."

"O Wafa," said one of the group of armed men which stood shivering on the beach in the cold hours of dawn, "may this be a good palaver! As for me, my stomach is filled with fearfulness. Let us all drink this magic water, for it gives us men courage."

"That you shall do when you have carried out all our master's works," said Wafa, and added with confidence: "Have no fear, for soon you shall see great wonders."

They heard the deep boom of the *Zaire*'s siren signalling a solitary and venturesome fisherman to quit the narrow fairway, and presently she came round the bend of the river, a dazzling white craft, showering sparks from her two slender smoke-stacks and leaving behind her twin cornucopias of grey smoke.

Wafa stepped into a canoe, and, seeing that the others were preparing to follow him, he struck out swiftly, manoeuvring his ironwood boat to the very waters from whence a scared fisherman was frantically paddling.

"Go not there, foreigner," wailed the Isisi Stabber-of-Waters, "for it is our lord Sandi, and his puc-a-puc has bellowed terribly."

"Die you!" roared Wafa. "On the river bottom your body, son of a fish and father of snakes!"

"O foreign frog!" came the shrill retort. "O poor man with two men's wives! O goatless – "

Wafa was too intent on his business to heed the rest. He struck the water strongly with his broad paddles, and reached the centre of the channel.

Bones of the Houssas put up his hand and jerked the rope of the siren.

*Whoo-o-o – woo-o-op!*

"Bless his silly old head," said Bones fretfully, "the dashed fellow will be run down!"

The girl was dusting Bones' cabin, and looked round. "What is it?" she asked.

Bones made no reply. He gripped the telegraph handle and rung the engines astern as Yoka, the steersman, spun the wheel.

Bump! Bump! Bumpily bump!

The steamer slowed and stopped, and the girl came out to the bridge in alarm. The *Zaire* had struck a sandbank, and was stranded high, if not dry.

"Bring that man on board," said the wrathful Bones. And they hauled to his presence Wafa, who was neither Arab nor N'gombi, but combined the vices of both.

"O man," said Bones, glaring at the offender through his eyeglass, "what evil ju-ju sent you to stop my fine ship?" He spoke in the Isisi dialect, and was surprised to be answered in coast Arabic.

"Lord," said the man, unmoved by the wrath of his overlord, "I come to make a great palaver concerning spirits and devils. Lord, I have found a great magic."

Bones grinned, for he had that sense of humour which rises superior to all other emotions. "Then you shall try your magic, my man, and lift this ship to deep water."

Wafa was not at all embarrassed. "Lord, this is a greater magic, for it concerns men, and brings to life the dead. For, lord, in this forest is a wonderful tree. Behold!"

He took from his loose-rolled waistband a piece of wood. Bones took it in his hand. It was the size of a corn cob, and had been newly cut, so that the wood was moist with sap. Bones smelt it. There was a faint odour of resin and camphor. Patricia Hamilton smiled. It was so like Bones to be led astray by side issues.

"Where is the wonder, man, that you should drive my ship upon a sandbank! And who are these?" Bones pointed to six canoes, filled with men, approaching the *Zaire*. The man did not answer, but, taking the wood from Bones' hand, pulled a knife from his belt and whittled a shaving.

"Here, lord," he said, "is my fine magic. With this wood I can do many miracles, such as making sick men strong and the strong weak."

Bones heard the canoes bump against the side of the boat, but his mind was occupied with curiosity.

"Thus do I make my magic, Tibbetti," droned Wafa. He held the knife by the haft in the right hand, and the chip of wood in his left. The point of the knife was towards the white man's heart.

"Bones!" screamed the girl.

Bones jumped aside and struck out as the man lunged. His nobbly fist caught Wafa under the jaw, and the man stumbled and fell. At the same instant there was a yell from the lower deck, the sound of scuffling and a shot.

Bones jumped for the girl, thrust her into the cabin, sliding the steel door behind him. His two revolvers hung at the head of his bunk, and he slipped them out, gave a glance to see whether they were loaded, and pushed the door.

"Shut the door after me," he breathed.

The bridge deck was deserted, and Bones raced down the ladder to the iron deck. Two Houssas and half a dozen natives lay dead or dying. The remainder of the soldiers were fighting desperately with whatever weapons they found to their hands – for, with characteristic carefulness, they had laid their rifles away in oil, lest the river air rust them – and, save for the sentry, who used a rifle common to all, they were unarmed.

"O dogs!" roared Bones.

The invaders turned and faced the long-barrelled Webleys, and the fight was finished. Later, Wafa came to the bridge with bright steel manacles on his wrist. His companions in the mad adventure sat on the iron deck below, roped leg to leg, and listened with philosophic calm as the Houssa sentry drew lurid pictures of the fate which awaited them.

Bones sat in his deep chair, and the prisoner squatted before him. "You shall tell my lord Sandi why you did this wickedness," he said, "also, Wafa, what evil thought was in your mind."

"Lord," said Wafa cheerfully, "what good comes to me if I speak?" Something about the man's demeanour struck Bones as strange, and he rose and went close to him.

"I see," he said, with a tightened lip. "The palaver is finished."

They led the man away, and the girl, who had been a spectator, asked anxiously: "What is wrong, Bones?"

But the young man shook his head. "The breaking of all that Sanders has worked for," he said bitterly, and the very absence of levity in one whose heart was so young and gay struck a colder chill to the girl's heart than the yells of the warring N'gombi. For Sanders had a big place in Patricia Hamilton's life. In an hour the *Zaire* was refloated, and was going at full speed down stream.

Sanders held his court in the thatched palaver house between the Houssa guard-room and the little stockade prison at the river's edge – a prison hidden amidst the flowering shrubs and acacia trees.

Wafa was the first to be examined. "Lord," he said, without embarrassment, "I tell you this – that I will not speak of the great wonders which lay in my heart unless you give me a book* that I shall go free."

Sanders smiled unpleasantly. "By the Prophet, I say what is true," he began confidentially; and Wafa winced at the oath, for he knew that truth was coming, and truth of a disturbing character. "In this land I govern millions of men," said Sanders, speaking deliberately, "I and two white lords, I govern by fear, Wafa, because there is no love in simple native men, save a love for their own and their bellies."

"Lord, you speak truth," said Wafa, the superior Arab of him responding to the confidence.

"Now, if you make to kill the lord Tibbetti," Sanders went on, "and do your wickedness for secret reasons, must I not discover what is that secret, lest it mean that I lose my hold upon the lands I govern?"

"Lord, that is also true," said Wafa.

"For what is one life more or less," asked Sanders, "a suffering smaller or greater by the side of my millions and their good?"

"Lord, you are Suliman," said Wafa eagerly. "Therefore, if you let me go, who shall be the worse for it?"

Again Sanders smiled, that grim parting of lip to show his white teeth. "Yet you may lie, and, if I let you go, I have neither the truth nor your body. No. Wafa, you shall speak." He rose up from his chair. "Today you shall go to the Village of Irons," he said; "tomorrow I will come to you, and you shall answer my questions. And, if you will not speak, I shall light a little fire in your chest, and that fire shall not go out except when the breath goes from your body. This palaver is finished."

So they took Wafa away to the Village of Irons, where the evil men of the Territories worked with chains about their ankles for their many sins, and in the morning came Sanders.

"Speak, man," he said.

* A written promise.

139

Wafa stared with an effort of defiance, but his face was twitching, for he saw the soldiers driving pegs into the ground, preparatory to staking him out. "I will speak the truth," he said.

So they took him into a hut, and there Sanders sat with him alone for half an hour; and when the Commissioner came out, his face was drawn and grey. He beckoned to Hamilton, who came forward and saluted. "We will get back to headquarters," he said shortly, and they arrived two hours later.

Sanders sat in the little telegraph office, and the Morse sounder rattled and clacked for half an hour. Other sounders were at work elsewhere, delicate needles vacillated in cable offices, and an Under-Secretary was brought from the House of Commons to the bureau of the Prime Minister to answer a question.

At four o'clock in the afternoon came the message Sanders expected: "London says permit for Corklan forged. Arrest. Take extremest steps. Deal drastically, ruthlessly. Holding in residence three companies African Rifles and mountain battery support you. Good luck. Administration."

Sanders came out of the office, and Bones met him.

"Men all aboard, sir," he reported.

"We'll go," said Sanders.

He met the girl halfway to the quay. "I know it is something very serious," she said quietly; "you have all my thoughts." She put both her hands in his, and he took them. Then, without a word, he left her.

Mr P T Corklan sat before his new hut in the village of Fimini. In that hut – the greatest the N'gombi had ever seen – were stored hundreds of packages all well wrapped and sewn in native cloth.

He was not smoking a cigar, because his stock of cigars was running short, but he was chewing a toothpick, for these at a pinch, could be improvised. He called to his headman. "Wafa?" he asked.

"Lord, he will come, for he is very cunning," said the headman.

Mr Corklan grunted. He walked to the edge of the village, where the ground sloped down to a strip of vivid green rushes. "Tell me, how long will this river be full?" he asked.

"Lord, for a moon."

Corklan nodded. Whilst the secret river ran, there was escape for him, for its meandering course would bring him and his rich cargo to Spanish territory and deep water.

His headman waited as though he had something to say.

"Lord," he said at last, "the chief of the N'coro village sends this night ten great teeth and a pot."

Corklan nodded. "If we're here, we'll get 'em. I hope we shall be gone."

And then the tragically unexpected happened. A man in white came through the trees towards him, and behind was another white man and a platoon of native soldiers.

"Trouble," said Corklan to himself, and thought the moment was one which called for a cigar.

"Good morning, Mr Sanders!" he said cheerfully.

Sanders eyed him in silence.

"This is an unexpected pleasure," said Corklan.

"Corklan, where is your still?" asked Sanders.

The plump man laughed. "You'll find it way back in the forest," he said, "and enough sweet potatoes to distil fifty gallons of spirit – all proof, sir, decimal 1986 specific gravity water extracted by Soemmering's method – in fact, as good as you could get it in England."

Sanders nodded. "I remember now – you're the man that ran the still in the Ashanti country, and got away with the concession."

"That's me," said the other complacently. "P T Corklan – I never assume an alias."

Sanders nodded again. "I came past villages," he said, "where every man and almost every woman was drunk. I have seen villages wiped out in drunken fights. I have seen a year's hard work ahead of me. You have corrupted a province in a very short space of time, and, as far as I can judge, you hoped to steal a Government ship and get into neutral territory with the prize you have won by your –"

"Enterprise," said Mr Corklan obligingly. "You'll have to prove that – about the ship. I am willing to stand any trial you like. There's no law about prohibition – it's one you've made yourself. I brought up the still – that's true – brought it up in sections and fitted it. I've been distilling spirits – that's true – "

"I also saw a faithful servant of Government, one Ali Kano," said Sanders, in a low voice. "He was lying on the bank of this secret river of yours with two revolver bullets in him."

"The nigger was spying on me, and I shot him," explained Corklan.

"I understand," said Sanders. And then, after a little pause: "Will you be hung or shot?"

The cigar dropped from the man's mouth. "Hey?" he said hoarsely. "You – you can't – do that – for making a drop of liquor – for niggers!"

"For murdering a servant of the State," corrected Sanders. "But, if it is any consolation to you, I will tell you that I would have killed you, anyway."

It took Mr Corklan an hour to make up his mind, and then he chose rifles.

Today the N'gombi point to a mound near the village of Fimini, which they call by a name which means, "The Waters of Madness," and it is believed to be haunted by devils.

# EYE TO EYE

"Bones," said Captain Hamilton, in despair, "you will never be a Napoleon."

"Dear old sir and brother-officer," said Lieutenant Tibbetts, "you are a jolly old pessimist."

Bones was by way of being examined in subjects C and D, for promotion to captaincy, and Hamilton was the examining officer. By all the rules and laws and strict regulations which govern military examinations, Bones had not only failed, but he had seriously jeopardized his right to his lieutenancy, if every man had his due.

"Now let me put this," said Hamilton. "Suppose you were in charge of a company of men, and you were attacked on three sides, and you had a river behind you on the fourth side, and you found things were going very hard against you. What would you do?"

"Dear old sir," said Bones thoughtfully, and screwing his face into all manner of contortions in his effort to secure the right answer, "I should go away and wet my heated brow in the purling brook, then I'd take counsel with myself."

"You'd lose," said Hamilton, with a groan. "That's the last person in the world you should go to for advice, Bones. Suppose," he said, in a last desperate effort to awaken a gleam of military intelligence in his subordinate's mind, "suppose you were trekking through the forest with a hundred rifles, and you found your way barred by a thousand armed men. What would you do?"

"Go back," said Bones, "and jolly quick, dear old fellow."

"Go back? What would you go back for?" asked the other, in astonishment.

"To make my will," said Bones firmly, "and to write a few letters to dear old friends in the far homeland. I have friends, Ham," he said, with dignity, "jolly old people who listen for my footsteps, and to whom my voice is music, dear old fellow."

"What other illusions do they suffer from?" asked Hamilton offensively, closing his book with a bang. "Well, you will be sorry to learn that I shall not recommend you for promotion."

"You don't mean that," said Bones hoarsely.

"I do mean that," said Hamilton.

"Well, I thought if I had a pal to examine me, I would go through with flying colours."

"Then I am not a pal. You don't suggest," said Hamilton, with ominous dignity, "that I would defraud the public by lying as to the qualities of a deficient character?"

"Yes, I do," said Bones, nodding vigorously, "for my sake and for the sake of the child." The child was that small native whom Bones had rescued and adopted.

"Not even for the sake of the child," said Hamilton, with an air of finality. "Bones, you're ploughed."

Bones did not speak, and Hamilton gathered together the papers, forms, and paraphernalia of examination.

He lifted his head suddenly, to discover that Bones was staring at him. It was no ordinary stare, but something that was a little uncanny. "What the dickens are you looking at?"

Bones did not speak. His round eyes were fixed on his superior in an unwinking glare.

"When I said you had failed," said Hamilton kindly, "I meant, of course – "

"That I'd passed," muttered Bones excitedly. "Say it, Ham – say it! 'Bones, congratulations, dear old lad' – "

"I meant," said Hamilton coldly, "that you have another chance next month."

The face of Lieutenant Tibbetts twisted into a painful contortion. "It didn't work!" he said bitterly, and stalked from the room.

"Rum beggar!" thought Hamilton, and smiled to himself.

"Have you noticed anything strange about Bones?" asked Patricia Hamilton the next day.

Her brother looked at her over his newspaper. "The strangest thing about Bones is Bones," he said, "and that I am compelled to notice every day of my life."

She looked up at Sanders, who was idly pacing the stoep of the Residency. "Have you, Mr Sanders?"

Sanders paused. "Beyond the fact that he is rather preoccupied and stares at one – "

"That is it," said the girl. "I knew I was right – he stares horribly. He has been doing it for a week – just staring. Do you think he is ill?"

"He has been moping in his hut for the past week," said Hamilton thoughtfully, "but I was hoping that it meant that he was swotting for his exam. But staring – I seem to remember – "

The subject of his discussion made his appearance at the far end of the square at that moment, and they watched him. First he walked slowly towards the Houssa sentry, who shouldered his arms in salute. Bones halted before the soldier and stared at him. Somehow, the watchers on the stoep knew that he was staring – there was something so fixed, so tense in his attitude. Then, without warning, the sentry's hand passed across his body, and the rifle came down to the "present."

"What on earth is he doing?" demanded the outraged Hamilton, for sentries do not present arms to subaltern officers.

Bones passed on. He stopped before one of the huts in the married lines, and stared at the wife of Sergeant Abiboo. He stared long and earnestly, and the woman, giggling uncomfortably, stared back. Then she began to dance.

"For Heaven's sake – " gasped Sanders, as Bones passed on.

"Bones!" roared Hamilton.

Bones turned first his head, then his body towards the Residency, and made his slow way towards the group.

"What is happening?" asked Hamilton.

The face of Bones was flushed; there was triumph in his eye – triumph which his pose of nonchalance could not wholly conceal. "What is happening, dear old officer?" he asked innocently, and stared.

"What the dickens are you goggling at?" demanded Hamilton irritably. "And please explain why you told the sentry to present arms to you."

"I didn't tell him, dear old sir and superior captain," said Bones. His eyes never left Hamilton's; he stared with a fierceness and with an intensity that was little short of ferocious.

"Confound you, what are you staring at? Aren't you well?" demanded Hamilton wrathfully.

Bones blinked. "Quite well, sir and comrade," he said gravely. "Pardon the question – did you feel a curious and unaccountable inclination to raise your right hand and salute me?"

"Did I – what?" demanded his dumbfounded superior.

"A sort of itchin' of the right arm – an almost overpowerin' inclination to touch your hat to poor old Bones?"

Hamilton drew a long breath. "I felt an almost overpowering desire to lift my foot," he said significantly.

"Look at me again," said Bones calmly. "Fix your eyes on mine an' think of nothin'. Now shut your eyes. Now you can't open 'em."

"Of course I can open them," said Hamilton. "Have you been drinking, Bones?"

A burst of delighted laughter from the girl checked Bones' indignant denial. "I know!" she cried, clapping her hands. "Bones is trying to mesmerize you!"

"What?"

The scarlet face of Bones betrayed him.

"Power of the human eye, dear old sir," he said hurriedly. "Some people have it – it's a gift. I discovered it the other day after readin' an article in *The Scientific Healer*."

"Phew!" Hamilton whistled. "So," he said, with dangerous calm, "all this staring and gaping of yours means that, does it? I remember now. When I was examining you for promotion the other day, you stared. Trying to mesmerize me?"

"Let bygones be bygones, dear old friend," begged Bones.

"And when I asked you to produce the company paysheets, which you forgot to bring up to date, you stared at me!"

"It's a gift," said Bones feebly.

"Oh, Bones," said the girl slowly, "you stared at me, too, after I refused to go picnicking with you on the beach."

"All's fair in love an' war," said Bones vaguely. "It's a wonderful gift."

"Have you ever mesmerized anybody?" asked Hamilton curiously, and Bones brightened up.

"Rather, dear old sir," he said. "Jolly old Ali, my secretary – goes off in a regular trance on the slightest provocation. Fact, dear old Ham."

Hamilton clapped his hands, and his orderly, dozing in the shade of the verandah, rose up. "Go, bring Ali Abid," said Hamilton. And when the man had gone: "Are you under the illusion that you made the sentry present arms to you, and Abiboo's woman dance for you, by the magic of your eye?"

"You saw," said the complacent Bones. "It's a wonderful gift, dear old Ham. As soon as I read the article, I tried it on Ali. Got him, first pop!"

The girl was bubbling with suppressed laughter, and there was a twinkle in Sanders' eye. "I recall that you saw me in connection with shooting leave in the N'gombi."

"Yes, sir and Excellency," said the miserable Bones.

"And I said that I thought it inadvisable, because of the trouble in the bend of the Isisi River."

"Yes, Excellency and sir," agreed Bones dolefully.

"And then you stared."

"Did I, dear old – Did I, sir?"

His embarrassment was relieved by the arrival of Ali. So buoyant a soul had Bones, that from the deeps of despair into which he was beginning to sink he rose to heights of confidence, not to say self-assurance, that were positively staggering.

"Miss Patricia, ladies and gentlemen," said Bones briskly, "we have here Ali Abid, confidential servant and faithful retainer. I will now endeavour to demonstrate the power of the human eye."

He met the stolid gaze of Ali and stared. He stared terribly and alarmingly, and Ali, to do him justice, stared back.

"Close your eyes," commanded Bones. "You can't open them, can you?"

"Sir," said Ali, "optics of subject are hermetically sealed."

"I will now put him in a trance," said Bones, and waved his hand mysteriously. Ali rocked backward and forward, and would have fallen but for the supporting arm of the demonstrator. "He is now insensible to pain," said Bones proudly.

"Lend me your hatpin, Pat," said Hamilton.

"I will now awaken him," said Bones hastily, and snapped his fingers. Ali rose to his feet with great dignity. "Thank you, Ali; you may go," said his master, and turned, ready to receive the congratulations of the party.

"Do you seriously believe that you mesmerized that humbug?"

Bones drew himself erect. "Sir and captain," he said stiffly, "do you suggest I am a jolly old impostor? You saw the sentry, sir, you saw the woman, sir."

"And I saw Ali," said Hamilton, nodding, "and I'll bet he gave the sentry something and the woman to play the goat for you."

Bones bowed slightly and distantly. "I cannot discuss my powers, dear old sir; you realize that there are some subjects too delicate to broach except with kindred spirits. I shall continue my studies of psychic mysteries undeterred by the cold breath of scepticism." He saluted everybody, and departed with chin up and shoulders squared, a picture of offended dignity.

That night Sanders lay in bed, snuggled up on his right side, which meant that he had arrived at the third stage of comfort which precedes that fading away of material life which men call sleep. Half consciously he listened to the drip, drip, drip of rain on the stoep, and promised himself that he would call upon Abiboo in the morning, to explain the matter of a choked gutter, for Abiboo had sworn, by the

Prophet and certain minor relatives of the Great One, that he had cleared every bird's nest from the ducts about the Residency.

Drip, drip, drip, drip, drip!

Sanders sank with luxurious leisure into the nothingness of the night.

Drip-tap, drip-tap, drip-tap!

He opened his eyes slowly, slid one leg out of bed, and groped for his slippers. He slipped into the silken dressing-gown which had been flung over the end of the bed, corded it about him, and switched on the electric light. Then he passed out into the big common room, with its chairs drawn together in overnight comradeship, and the solemn tick of the big clock to emphasize the desolation. He paused a second to switch on the lights, then went to the door and flung it open.

"Enter!" he said in Arabic.

The man who came in was naked, save for a tarboosh on his head and a loincloth about his middle. His slim body shone with moisture, and where he stood on the white matting were two little pools. Kano from his brown feet to the soaked fez, he stood erect with that curious assumption of pride and equality which the Mussulman bears with less offence to his superiors than any other race.

"Peace on this house," he said, raising his hand.

"Speak, Ahmet," said Sanders, dropping into a big chair and stretched back, with his clasped hands behind his head. He eyed the man gravely and without resentment, for no spy would tap upon his window at night save that the business was a bad one.

"Lord," said the man, "it is shameful that I should wake your lordship from your beautiful dream, but I came with the river."* He looked down at his master, and in the way of certain Kano people, who are dialecticians to a man, he asked: "Lord, it is written in the Sura of Ya-Sin, 'To the sun it is not given to overtake the moon – "

" 'Nor doth the night outstrip the day; but each in his own sphere doth journey on,' " finished Sanders patiently. "Thus also begins the

---

* I came when I could.

Sura of the Cave: 'Praise be to God, Who hath sent down the book to his servant, and hath put no crookedness into it.' Therefore, Ahmet, be plain to me, and leave your good speeches till you meet the abominable Sufi."

The man sank to his haunches. "Lord," he said, "from the bend of the river, where the Isisi divides the land of the N'gombi from the lands of the Good Chief, I came, travelling by day and night with the river, for many strange things have happened which are too wonderful for me. This Chief Busesi, whom all men call good, has a daughter by his second wife. In the year of the High Crops she was given to a stranger from the forest, him they call Gufuri-Bululu, and he took her away to live in his hut."

Sanders sat up. "Go on, man," he said.

"Lord, she has returned and performs wonderful magic," said the man, "for by the wonder of her eyes she can make dead men live and live men die, and all people are afraid. Also, lord, there was a wise man in the forest, who was blind, and he had a daughter who was the prop and staff of him, and because of his wisdom, and because she hated all who rivalled her, the woman D'rona Gufuri told certain men to seize the girl and hold her in a deep pool of water until she was dead."

"This is a bad palaver," said Sanders; "but you shall tell me what you mean by the wonder of her eyes."

"Lord," said the man, "she looks upon men, and they do her will. Now, it is her will that there shall be a great dance on the Rind of the Moon, and after she shall send the spears of the people of Busesi – who is old and silly, and for this reason is called good – against the N'gombi folk."

"Oh," said Sanders, biting his lip in thought, "by the wonder of her eyes!"

"Lord," said the man, "even I have seen this, for she has stricken men to the ground by looking at them, and some she has made mad, and others foolish."

Sanders turned his head at a noise from the doorway. The tall figure of Hamilton stood peering sleepily at the light.

"I heard your voice," he said apologetically. "What is the trouble?"

Briefly Sanders related the story the man had told.

"Wow!" said Hamilton, in a paroxysm of delight.

"What's wrong?"

"Bones!" shouted Hamilton. "Bones is the fellow. Let him go up and subdue her with his eye. He's the very fellow. I'll go over and call him, sir."

He hustled into his clothing, slipped on a mackintosh, and, making his way across the dark square, admitted himself to the sleeping-hut of Lieutenant Tibbetts. By the light of his electric torch he discovered the slumberer. Bones lay on his back, his large mouth wide open, one thin leg thrust out from the covers, and he was making strange noises. Hamilton found the lamp and lit it, then he proceeded to the heart-breaking task of waking his subordinate. "Up, you lazy devil!" he shouted, shaking Bones by the shoulder.

Bones opened his eyes and blinked rapidly. "On the word 'One!'" he said hoarsely, "carry the left foot ten inches to the left front, at the same time bringing the rifle to a horizontal position at the right side. One!"

"Wake up, wake up, Bones!"

Bones made a wailing noise. It was the noise of a mother panther who has returned to her lair to discover that her offspring have been eaten by wild pigs. "Whar-r-ow-ow!" he said, and turned over on his right side.

Hamilton pocketed his torch, and, lifting Bones bodily from the bed, let him fall with a thud.

Bones scrambled up, staring. "Gentlemen of the jury," he said, "I stand before you a ruined man. Drink has been my downfall, as the dear old judge remarked. I *did* kill Wilfred Morgan, and I plead the unwritten law." He saluted stiffly, collapsed on to his pillow, and fell instantly into a deep child-like sleep.

Hamilton groaned. He had had occasion to wake Bones from his beauty sleep before, but he had never been as bad as this. He took a soda siphon from the little sideboard and depressed the lever, holding the outlet above his victim's head.

Bones leapt up with a roar. "Hello, Ham!" he said quite sanely. "Well dear old officer, this is the finish! You stand by the lifeboat an' shoot down anybody who attempts to leave the ship before the torpedoes are saved. I'm goin' down into the hold to have a look at the women an' children." He saluted, and was stepping out into the wet night, when Hamilton caught his arm.

"Steady, the Buffs, my sleeping beauty! Dress yourself. Sanders wants you."

Bones nodded. "I'll just drive over and see him," he said, climbed back into bed, and was asleep in a second.

Hamilton put out the light and went back to the Residency. "I hadn't the heart to cut his ear off," he said regretfully. "I'm afraid we shan't be able to consult Bones till the morning."

Sanders nodded. "Anyway, I will wait for the morning. I have told Abiboo to get stores and wood aboard, and to have steam in the *Zaire*. Let us emulate Bones."

"Heaven forbid!" said Hamilton piously.

Bones came blithely to breakfast, a dapper and a perfectly groomed figure. He received the news of the ominous happenings in the N'gombi country with that air of profound solemnity which so annoyed Hamilton.

"I wish you had called me in the night," he said gravely. "Dear old officer, I think it was due to me."

"Called you! Called you! Why – why – " spluttered Hamilton.

"In fact we did call you, Bones, but we could not wake you," smoothed Sanders.

A look of youthful amazement spread over the youthful face of Lieutenant Tibbetts. "You called me?" he asked incredulously. "Called *me*?"

"*You!*" hissed Hamilton. "I not only called you, but I kicked you. I poured water on you, and I chucked you up to the roof of the hut and dropped you."

A faint but unbelieving smile from Bones. "Are you sure it was me, dear old officer?" he asked, and Hamilton choked. "I only ask," said

Bones, turning blandly to the girl, "because I'm a notoriously light sleeper, dear old Miss Patricia. The slightest stir wakes me, and instantly I'm in possession of all my faculties. Bosambo calls me 'Eye-That-Never-Shuts – ' "

"Bosambo is a notorious leg-puller," interrupted Hamilton irritably. "Really, Bones – "

"Often, dear old Sister," Bones went on impressively, "campin' out in the forest, an' sunk in the profound sleep which youth an' good conscience brings, something has wakened me, an' I've jumped to my feet, a revolver in my hand, an' what do you think it was?"

"A herd of wild elephants walking on your chest?" suggested Hamilton.

"What do you think it was, dear old Patricia miss?" persisted Bones, and interrupted her ingenious speculation in his usual aggravating manner: "The sound of a footstep breakin' a twig a hundred yards away!"

"Wonderful!" sneered Hamilton, stirring his coffee. "Bones, if you could only spell, what a novelist you'd be!"

"The point is," said Sanders, with good-humoured patience, which brought, for some curious reason, a warm sense of intimacy to the girl, "you've got to go up and try your eye on the woman D'rona Gufuri."

Bones leaned back in his chair and spoke with deliberation and importance, for he realized that he, and only he, could supply a solution to the difficulties of his superiors.

"The power of the human eye, when applied by a jolly old scientist to a heathen, is irresistible. You may expect me down with the prisoner in four days."

"She may be more trouble than you expect," said Sanders seriously. "The longer one lives in native lands, the less confident one can be. There have been remarkable cases of men possessing the power which this woman has – "

"And which I have, sir an' Excellency, to an extraordinary extent," interrupted Bones firmly. "Have no fear."

Thirty-six hours later Bones stood before the woman D'rona Gufuri.

"Lord," said the woman, "men speak evilly of me to Sandi, and now you have come to take me to the Village of Irons."

"That is true, D'rona," said Bones, and looked into her eyes.

"Lord," said the woman, speaking slowly, "you shall go back to Sandi and say, 'I have not seen the woman D'rona' – for, lord, is this not truth?"

"I'wa! I'wa!" muttered Bones thickly.

"You cannot see me, Tibbetti, and I am not here," said the woman, and she spoke before the assembled villagers, who stood, knuckles to teeth, gazing awe-stricken upon the scene.

"I cannot see you," said Bones sleepily.

"And now you cannot hear me, lord?"

Bones did not reply.

The woman took him by the arm and led him through the patch of wood which fringes the river and separated beach from village. None followed them; even the two Houssas who formed the escort of Lieutenant Tibbetts stayed rooted to the spot.

Bones passed into the shadow of the trees, the woman's hand on his arm. Then suddenly from the undergrowth rose a lank figure, and D'rona of the Magic Eye felt a bony hand at her throat. She laughed.

"O man, whoever you be, look upon me in this light, and your strength shall melt."

She twisted round to meet her assailant's face, and shrieked aloud, for he was blind. And Bones stood by without moving, without seeing or hearing, whilst the strong hands of the blind witch-doctor, whose daughter she had slain, crushed the life from her body.

"Of course sir," explained Bones, "you may think she mesmerized me. On the other hand, it is quite possible that she acted under my influence. It's a moot point, sir an' Excellency – jolly moot!"

# THE HOODED KING

There was a certain Portuguese governor – this was in the days when Colhemos was Colonial Minister – who had a small legitimate income and an extravagant wife. This good lady had a villa at Cintra, a box at the Real Theatre de São Carlos, and a motor-car, and gave five o'clocks at the Hotel Nunes to the aristocracy and gentry who inhabited that spot, of whom the ecstatic Spaniard said, "dejar a Cintra, y ver al mundo entero, es, con verdad caminar en capuchera."

Since her husband's salary was exactly $66.50 weekly and the upkeep of the villa alone was twice that amount, it is not difficult to understand that Senhor Bonaventura was a remarkable man.

Colhemos came over to the Foreign Office in the Praco de Commercio one day and saw Dr Sarabesta, and Sarabesta, who was both a republican and a sinner, was also ambitious, or he had a Plan and an Ideal – two very dangerous possessions for a politician, since they lead inevitably to change, than which nothing is more fatal to political systems.

"Colhemos," said the doctor dramatically, "you are ruining me! You are bringing me to the dust and covering me with the hatred and mistrust of the Powers!"

He folded his arms and rose starkly from the chair, his beard all a-bristle, his deep little eyes glaring.

"What is wrong, Baptista?" asked Colhemos.

The other flung out his arms in an extravagant gesture.

"Ruin!" he cried, somewhat inadequately.

He opened the leather portfolio which lay on the table and extracted six sheets of foolscap paper.

"Read!" he said, and subsided into his padded armchair a picture of gloom.

The sheets of foolscap were surmounted by crests showing an emaciated lion and a small horse with a spiral horn in his forehead endeavouring to climb a chafing-dish which had been placed on edge for the purpose, and was suitably inscribed with another lion, two groups of leopards and a harp.

Colhemos did not stop to admire the menagerie, but proceeded at once to the literature. It was in French, and had to do with a certain condition of affairs in Portuguese Central Africa which "constituted a grave and increasing menace to the native subjects" of "Grande Bretagne." There were hints, "which His Majesty's Government would be sorry to believe, of raids and requisitions upon the native manhood" of this country which differed little from slave raids.

Further, "Mr Commissioner Sanders of the Territories regretted to learn" that these labour requisitions resulted in a condition of affairs not far removed from slavery.

Colhemos read through the dispatch from start to finish, and put it down thoughtfully.

"Pinto has been overdoing it," he admitted. "I shall have to write to him."

"What you write to Pinto may be interesting enough to print," said Dr Sarabesta violently, "but what shall I write to London? This Commissioner Sanders is a fairly reliable man, and his Government will act upon what he says."

Colhemos, who was really a great man (it was a distinct loss when he faced a firing platoon in the revolutionary days of '12), tapped his nose with a penholder.

"You can say that we shall send a special commissioner to the M'fusi country to report, and that he will remain permanently established in the M'fusi to suppress lawless acts."

The doctor looked up wonderingly.

"Pinto won't like that," said he, "besides which, the M'fusi are quite unmanageable. The last time we tried to bring them to reason it cost – Santa Maria!…and the lives!…phew!"

Colhemos nodded.

"The duc de Sagosta," he said slowly, "is an enthusiastic young man. He is also a royalist and allied by family ties to Dr Ceillo of the Left. He is, moreover, an Anglomaniac – though why he should be when his mother was an American woman, I do not know. He shall be our commissioner, my dear Baptista."

His dear Baptista sat bolt upright, every hair in his bristling head erect.

"A royalist!" he gasped, "do you want to set Portugal ablaze?"

"There are moments when I could answer 'Yes' to that question," said the truthful Colhemos, "but for the moment I am satisfied that there will be no fireworks. It will do no harm to send the boy. It will placate the Left and please the Clerics – it will also consolidate our reputation for liberality and largeness of mind. Also the young man will either be killed or fall a victim to the sinister influences of that corruption which, alas, has also entered into the vitals of our Colonial service."

So Manuel duc de Sagosta was summoned, and prepared for the subject of his visit by telephone, came racing up from Cintra in his big American juggernaut, leapt up the stairs of the Colonial Office two at a time, and came to Colhemos' presence in a state of mind which may be described as a big mental whoop.

"You will understand, Senhor," said Colhemos, "that I am doing that which may make me unpopular. For that I care nothing! My country is my first thought, and the glory and honour of our flag! Some day you may hold my portfolio in the Cabinet, and it will be well if you bring to your high and noble office the experience…"

Then they all talked together, and the dark room flickered with gesticulating palms.

Colhemos came to see the boy off by the MNP boat which carried him to the African Coast.

157

"I suppose, Senhor," said the duc, "there would be no objection on the part of the Government to my calling on my way at a certain British port. I have a friend in the English army – we were at Clifton together – "

"My friend," said Colhemos, pressing the young man's hand warmly, "you must look upon England as a potential ally, and lose no opportunity which offers to impress upon our dear colleagues this fact, that behind England, unmoved, unshaken, faithful, stands the armed might of Portugal. May the saints have you in their keeping!"

He embraced him, kissing him on both cheeks.

Bones was drilling recruits at headquarters when Hamilton hailed him from the edge of the square.

"There's a pal of yours come to see you, Bones," he roared. Bones marched sedately to his superior and touched his helmet.

"Sir!"

"A friend of yours – just landed from the Portuguese packet."

Bones was mystified, and went up to the Residency to find a young man in spotless white being entertained by Patricia Hamilton and a very thoughtful Sanders.

The duc de Sagosta leapt to his feet as Bones came up the verandah.

"Hullo, Conk!" he yelled hilariously.

Bones stared.

"God bless my life," he stammered, "it's Mug!"

There was a terrific hand-shaking accompanied by squawking inquiries which were never answered, uproarious laughter, back patting, brazen and baseless charges that each was growing fat, and Sanders watched it with great kindness.

"Here's old Ham," said Bones, "you ought to know Ham – Captain Hamilton, sir, my friend, the duke of something or other – but you can call him Mug – Miss Hamilton – this is Mug."

"We've already been introduced," she laughed. "But why do you let him call you Mug?"

The duc grinned.

158

"I like Mug," he said simply.

He was to stay for lunch, for the ship was not leaving until the afternoon, and Bones carried him off to his hut.

"A joyous pair," said Hamilton enviously. "Lord, if I was only a boy again!"

Sanders shook his head.

"You don't echo that wish?" said Pat.

"I wasn't thinking about that – I was thinking of the boy. I dislike this M'fusi business, and I can't think why the Government sent him. They are a pretty bad lot – their territory is at the back of the Akasava, and the Chief of the M'fusi is a rascal."

"But he says that he has been sent to reform them," said the girl.

Sanders smiled.

"It is not a job I should care to undertake – and yet – "

He knitted his forehead.

"And yet – ?"

"I could reform them – Bones could reform them. But if they were reformed it would break Bonaventura, for he holds his job subject to their infamy."

At lunch Sanders was unusually silent, a silence which was unnoticed, save by the girl. Bones and his friend, however, needed no stimulation. Lunch was an almost deafening meal, and when the time came for the duc to leave, the whole party went down to the beach to see him embark.

"Goodbye, old Mug!" roared Bones, as the boat pulled away. "Whoop! hi! how!"

"You're a noisy devil," said Hamilton, admiringly.

"Vox populi, vox Dei," said Bones.

He had an unexpected visitor that evening, for whilst he was dressing for dinner, Sanders came into his hut – an unusual happening.

What Sanders had to say may not be related since it was quite unofficial, but Bones came to dinner that night and behaved with such decorum and preserved a mien so grave, that Hamilton thought he was ill.

The duc continued his journey down the African Coast and presently came to a port which was little more than a beach, a jetty, a big white house, and by far the most imposing end of the Moanda road. In due time, he arrived by the worst track in the world (he was six days on the journey) at Moanda itself, and came into the presence of the Governor.

Did the duc but know it, his Excellency had also been prepared for the young man's mission. The mail had arrived by carrier the day before the duc put in his appearance, and Pinto Bonaventura had his little piece all ready to say.

"I will give you all the assistance I possibly can," he said, as they sat at *déjeuner*, "but, naturally, I cannot guarantee your immunity."

"Immunity?" said the puzzled duc.

Senhor Bonaventura nodded gravely.

"Nothing is more repugnant to me than slavery," he said, "unless it be the terrible habit of drinking. If I could sweep these evils out of existence with a wave of my hand, believe me I would do so; but I cannot perform miracles, and the Government will not give me sufficient troops to suppress these practices which every one of us hold in abhorrence."

"But," protested the duc, a little alarmed, "since I am going to reform the M'fusi…"

The Governor choked over his coffee and apologized. He did not laugh, because long residence in Central Africa had got him out of the habit, and had taught him a certain amount of self-control in all things except the consumption of marsala.

"Pray go on," he said, wearing an impassive face.

"It will be to the interests of Portugal, no less than to your Excellency's interest," said the young man, leaning across the table and speaking with great earnestness, "if I can secure a condition of peace, prosperity, sobriety, and if I can establish the Portuguese law in this disturbed area."

"Undoubtedly," acknowledged the older man with profound seriousness.

So far from the duc's statement representing anything near the truth, it may be said that a restoration of order would serve his Excellency very badly indeed. In point of fact he received something like eight shillings for every "head" of "recruited labour." He also received a commission from the same interested syndicates which exported able-bodied labourers, a commission amounting to six shillings upon every case of square-face, and a larger sum upon every keg of rum that came into the country.

Sobriety and law would, in fact, spell much discomfort to the elegant lady who lived in the villa at Cintra, and would considerably diminish not only Senhor Bonaventura's handsome balance at the Bank of Brazil, but would impoverish certain ministers, permanent and temporary, who looked to their dear Pinto for periodical contributions to what was humorously described as "The Party Fund."

Yet the duc de Sagosta went into the wilds with a high heart and a complete faith, in his youthful and credulous soul, that he had behind him the full moral and physical support of a high-minded and patriotic Governor. The high-minded and patriotic Governor, watching the caravan of his new assistant disappearing through the woods which fringe Moanda, expressed in picturesque language his fervent hope that the mud, the swamp, the forest and the wilderness of the M'fusi country would swallow up this young man for evermore, amen. The unpopularity of the new Commissioner was sealed when the Governor learnt of his visit to Sanders, for "Sanders" was a name at which his Excellency made disapproving noises.

The predecessor of the duc de Sagosta was dead. His grave was in the duc's front garden, and was covered with rank grass. The newcomer found the office correspondence in order (as a glib native clerk demonstrated); he also found 103 empty bottles behind the house, and understood the meaning of that coarse grave in the garden. He found that the last index number in the letter book was 951.

It is remarkable that the man he succeeded should have found, in one year, 951 subjects for correspondence, but it is the fact. Possibly nine hundred of the letters had to do with the terrible state of the

Residency at Uango-Bozeri. The roof leaked, the foundations had settled, and not a door closed as it should close. On the day of his arrival the duc found a *mamba* resting luxuriously in his one armchair, a discovery which suggested the existence of a whole colony of these deadly brutes – the *mamba* bite is fatal in exactly ninety seconds – under or near the house.

The other fifty dispatches probably had to do with the late Commissioner's arrears of pay, for Portugal at that time was in the throes of her annual crisis, and ministries were passing through the Government offices at Lisbon with such rapidity that before a cheque could be carried from the Foreign Office to the bank, it was out of date.

Uango-Bozeri is 220 miles by road from the coast, and is the centre of the child-like people of the M'fusi. Here the duc dwelt and had his being, as Governor of 2,000 square miles, and overlord of some million people who were cannibals with a passion for a fiery liquid which was described by traders as "rum." It was as near rum as the White City is to Heaven; that is to say, to the uncultivated taste it might have been rum, and anyway was as near to rum as the taster could expect to get.

This is all there is to be said about the duc de Sagosta, save that his headman swindled him, his soldiers were conscienceless natives committing acts of brigandage in his innocent name, whilst his chief at Moanda was a peculating and incompetent scoundrel.

At the time when the duc was finding life a bitter and humiliating experience, and had reached the stage when he sat on his predecessor's grave for company, a small and unauthorized party crossed the frontier from the British Territories in search of adventure.

Now it happened that the particular region through which the border-line passed was governed by the Chief of the Greater M'fusi, who was a cannibal, a drunkard, and a master of two regiments.

The duc had been advised not to interfere with the chief of his people, and he had (after one abortive and painful experience) obeyed his superiors, accepting the hut tax which was sent to him (and which was obviously and insolently inadequate) without demur.

No white man journeyed to the city of the M'fusi without invitation from the chief, and as Chief Karata never issued such invitation, the Greater M'fusi was a *terra incognita* even to his Excellency the Governor-General of the Central and Western Provinces.

Karata was a drunkard approaching lunacy. It was his whim for weeks on end to wear on his head the mask of a goat. At other times, "as a mark of his confidence in devils," he would appear hidden beneath a plaited straw extinguisher which fitted him from head to foot. He was eccentric in other ways which need not be particularized, but he was never so eccentric that he welcomed strangers.

Unfortunately for those concerned, the high road from the Territories passed through the M'fusi drift. And one day there came a panting messenger from the keeper of the drift who flung himself down at the king's feet.

"Lord," said he, "there is a white man at the drift, and with him a certain chief and his men."

"You will take the men, bringing them to me tied with ropes," said the king, who looked at the messenger with glassy eyes and found some difficulty in speaking, for he was at the truculent stage of his second bottle.

The messenger returned and met the party on the road. What was his attitude towards the intruders it is impossible to say. He may have been insolent, secure in the feeling that he was representing his master's attitude towards white men; he may have offered fight in the illusion that the six warriors he took with him were sufficient to enforce the king's law. It is certain that he never returned.

Instead there came to the king's kraal a small but formidable party under a white man, and they arrived at a propitious moment, for the ground before the king's great hut was covered with square bottles, and the space in front of the palace was crowded with wretched men chained neck to neck and waiting to march to the coast and slavery.

The white man pushed back his helmet.

"Goodness gracious Heavens!" he exclaimed, "how perfectly horrid! Bosambo, this is immensely illegal an' terrificly disgustin'."

The Chief of the Ochori looked round.

"Dis feller be dam' bad," was his effort.

Bones walked leisurely to the shady canopy under which the king sat, and King Karata stared stupidly at the unexpected vision.

"O King," said Bones in the Akasavian vernacular which runs from Dacca to the Congo, "this is an evil thing you do – against all law."

Open-mouthed Karata continued to stare.

To the crowded kraal, on prisoner and warrior, councillor and dancing woman alike, came a silence deep and unbroken.

They heard the words spoken in a familiar tongue, and marvelled that a white man should speak it. Bones was carrying a stick and taking deliberate aim, and after two trial strokes he brought the nobbly end round with a "swish!"

A bottle of square-face smashed into a thousand pieces, and there arose on the hot air the sickly scent of crude spirits. Fascinated, silent, motionless, King Karata, named not without reason "The Terrible," watched the destruction as bottle followed bottle.

Then as a dim realization of the infamy filtered through his thick brain, he rose with a growl like a savage animal, and Bones turned quickly. But Bosambo was quicker. One stride brought him to the king's side.

"Down, dog!" he said. "O Kafata, you are very near the painted hut where dead kings lie."

The king sat back and glared to and fro.

All that was animal in him told of his danger; he smelt death in the mirthless grin of the white man; he smelt it as strongly under the hand of the tall native wearing the monkey-tails of chieftainship. If they would only stand away from him they would die quickly enough. Let them get out of reach, and a shout, an order, would send them bloodily to the ground with little kicks and twitches as the life ran out of them.

But they stood too close, and that order of his meant his death.

"O white man," he began.

"Listen, black man," said Bosambo, and lapsed into his English; "hark um, you dam' black nigger – what for you speak um so?"

"You shall say 'master' to me, Karata," said Bones easily, "for in my land 'white man' is evil talk." *

"Master," said the king sullenly, "this is a strange thing – for I see that you are English and we be servants of another king. Also it is forbidden that any white – that any master should stand in my kraal without my word, and I have driven even Igselensi from my face."

"That is all foolish talk, Karata," said Bones. "This is good talk: shall Karata live or shall he die? This you shall say. If you send away this palaver and say to your people that we are folk whom you desire shall live in the shadow of the king's hut, then you live. Let him say less than this, Bosambo, and you strike quickly."

The king looked from face to face. Bones had his hand in the uniform jacket pocket. Bosambo balanced his killing-spear on the palm of his hand, the chief saw with the eye of an expert that the edge was razor sharp.

Then he turned to the group whom Bones had motioned away when he started to speak to the king.

"This palaver is finished," he said, "and the white lord stays in my hut for a night."

"Good egg," said Bones as the crowd streamed from the kraal.

Senhor Bonaventura heard of the arrival of a white man at the chief's great kraal and was not perturbed, because there were certain favourite traders who came to the king from time to time. He was more concerned by the fact that a labour draft of eight hundred men who had been promised by Karata had not yet reached Moanda, but frantic panic came from the remarkable information of Karata's eccentricities which had reached him from his lieutenant.

The duc's letter may be reproduced.

---

* In most native countries "white man" is seldom employed save as a piece of insolence. It is equivalent to the practice of referring to the natives as niggers.

## ILLUSTRIOUS AND EXCELLENT SENHOR,

It is with joy that I announce to you the most remarkable reformation of King Karata. The news was brought to me that the king had received a number of visitors of an unauthorized character, and though I had, as I have reported to you, Illustrious and Excellent Senhor, the most unpleasant experience at the hands of the king, I deemed it advisable to go to the city of the Greater M'fusi and conduct an inquiry.

I learnt that the king had indeed received the visitors, and that they had departed on the morning of my arrival carrying with them one of their number who was sick. With this party was a white man. But the most remarkable circumstance, Illustrious and Excellent Senhor, was that the king had called a midnight palaver of his councillors and high people of state and had told them that the strangers had brought news of such sorrowful character that for four moons it would be forbidden to look upon his face. At the end of that period he would disappear from the earth and become a god amongst the stars.

At these words, Illustrious and Excellent Senhor, the king with some reluctance took from one of the strangers a bag in which two eyes had been cut, and pulled it over his head and went back into his hut.

Since then he has done many remarkable things. He has forbidden the importation of drink, and has freed all labour men to their homes. He has nominated Zifingini, the elder chief of the M'fusi, to be king after his departure, and has added another fighting regiment to his army.

He is quite changed, and though they cannot see his face and he has banished all his wives, relatives and councillors to a distant village, he is more popular than ever.

Illustrious and Excellent Senhor, I feel that at last I am seeing the end of the old regime and that we may look forward to a period of sobriety and prosperity in the M'fusi.

Receive the assurance, Illustrious and Excellent Senhor, of my distinguished consideration.

His Excellency went purple and white.

"Holy mother!" he spluttered apoplectically, "this is ruin!"

With trembling hands he wrote a telegram. Translated in its sense it was to this effect – "Recall de Sagosta without fail or there will be nothing doing on pay day."

He saw this dispatched on its way, and returned to his bureau. He picked up the duc's letter and read it again: then he saw there was a postscript.

PS – In regard to the strangers who visisted the king, the man they carried away on a closed litter was very sick indeed, according to the accounts of woodmen who met the party. He was raving at the top of his voice, but the white man was singing very loudly.

PPS – I have just heard, Illustrious and Excellent Senhor, that the Hooded King (as his people call him) has sent off all his richest treasures and many others which he has taken from the huts of his deported relatives to one Bosambo, who is a chief of the Ochori in British Territory, and is distantly related to Senhor Sanders, the Commissioner of that Territory.

# EDGAR WALLACE

## BIG FOOT

Footprints and a dead woman bring together Superintendent Minton and the amateur sleuth Mr Cardew. Who is the man in the shrubbery? Who is the singer of the haunting Moorish tune? Why is Hannah Shaw so determined to go to Pawsy, 'a dog lonely place' she had previously detested? Death lurks in the dark and someone must solve the mystery before BIG FOOT strikes again, in a yet more fiendish manner.

## BONES IN LONDON

The new Managing Director of Schemes Ltd has an elegant London office and a theatrically dressed assistant – however, Bones, as he is better known, is bored. Luckily there is a slump in the shipping market and it is not long before Joe and Fred Pole pay Bones a visit. They are totally unprepared for Bones' unnerving style of doing business, unprepared for his unique style of innocent and endearing mischief.

# EDGAR WALLACE

## BONES OF THE RIVER

'Taking the little paper from the pigeon's leg, Hamilton saw it was from Sanders and marked URGENT. *Send Bones instantly to Lujamalababa… Arrest and bring to headquarters the witch doctor.*'

It is a time when the world's most powerful nations are vying for colonial honour, a time of trading steamers and tribal chiefs. In the mysterious African territories administered by Commissioner Sanders, Bones persistently manages to create his own unique style of innocent and endearing mischief.

## THE DAFFODIL MYSTERY

When Mr Thomas Lyne, poet, poseur and owner of Lyne's Emporium insults a cashier, Odette Rider, she resigns. Having summoned detective Jack Tarling to investigate another employee, Mr Milburgh, Lyne now changes his plans. Tarling and his Chinese companion refuse to become involved. They pay a visit to Odette's flat and in the hall Tarling meets Sam, convicted felon and protégé of Lyne. Next morning Tarling discovers a body. The hands are crossed on the breast, adorned with a handful of daffodils.

# EDGAR WALLACE

## THE JOKER
### (USA: THE COLOSSUS)

While the millionaire Stratford Harlow is in Princetown, not only does he meet with his lawyer Mr Ellenbury but he gets his first glimpse of the beautiful Aileen Rivers, niece of the actor and convicted felon Arthur Ingle. When Aileen is involved in a car accident on the Thames Embankment, the driver is James Carlton of Scotland Yard. Later that evening Carlton gets a call. It is Aileen. She needs help.

## THE SQUARE EMERALD
### (USA: THE GIRL FROM SCOTLAND YARD)

'Suicide on the left,' says Chief Inspector Coldwell pleasantly, as he and Leslie Maughan stride along the Thames Embankment during a brutally cold night. A gaunt figure is sprawled across the parapet. But Coldwell soon discovers that Peter Dawlish, fresh out of prison for forgery, is not considering suicide but murder. Coldwell suspects Druze as the intended victim. Maughan disagrees. If Druze dies, she says, 'It will be because he does not love children!'

## OTHER TITLES BY EDGAR WALLACE AVAILABLE DIRECT
## FROM HOUSE OF STRATUS

| Quantity | | £ | $(US) | $(CAN) | € |
|---|---|---|---|---|---|
| | THE ADMIRABLE CARFEW | 6.99 | 12.95 | 19.95 | 13.50 |
| | THE ANGEL OF TERROR | 6.99 | 12.95 | 19.95 | 13.50 |
| | THE AVENGER (USA: THE HAIRY ARM) | 6.99 | 12.95 | 19.95 | 13.50 |
| | BARBARA ON HER OWN | 6.99 | 12.95 | 19.95 | 13.50 |
| | BIG FOOT | 6.99 | 12.95 | 19.95 | 13.50 |
| | THE BLACK ABBOT | 6.99 | 12.95 | 19.95 | 13.50 |
| | BONES | 6.99 | 12.95 | 19.95 | 13.50 |
| | BONES IN LONDON | 6.99 | 12.95 | 19.95 | 13.50 |
| | BONES OF THE RIVER | 6.99 | 12.95 | 19.95 | 13.50 |
| | THE CLUE OF THE NEW PIN | 6.99 | 12.95 | 19.95 | 13.50 |
| | THE CLUE OF THE SILVER KEY | 6.99 | 12.95 | 19.95 | 13.50 |
| | THE CLUE OF THE TWISTED CANDLE | 6.99 | 12.95 | 19.95 | 13.50 |
| | THE COAT OF ARMS | | | | |
| | (USA: THE ARRANWAYS MYSTERY) | 6.99 | 12.95 | 19.95 | 13.50 |
| | THE COUNCIL OF JUSTICE | 6.99 | 12.95 | 19.95 | 13.50 |
| | THE CRIMSON CIRCLE | 6.99 | 12.95 | 19.95 | 13.50 |
| | THE DAFFODIL MYSTERY | 6.99 | 12.95 | 19.95 | 13.50 |
| | THE DARK EYES OF LONDON | | | | |
| | (USA: THE CROAKERS) | 6.99 | 12.95 | 19.95 | 13.50 |
| | THE DAUGHTERS OF THE NIGHT | 6.99 | 12.95 | 19.95 | 13.50 |
| | A DEBT DISCHARGED | 6.99 | 12.95 | 19.95 | 13.50 |
| | THE DEVIL MAN | 6.99 | 12.95 | 19.95 | 13.50 |
| | THE DOOR WITH SEVEN LOCKS | 6.99 | 12.95 | 19.95 | 13.50 |
| | THE DUKE IN THE SUBURBS | 6.99 | 12.95 | 19.95 | 13.50 |
| | THE FACE IN THE NIGHT | 6.99 | 12.95 | 19.95 | 13.50 |
| | THE FEATHERED SERPENT | 6.99 | 12.95 | 19.95 | 13.50 |
| | THE FLYING SQUAD | 6.99 | 12.95 | 19.95 | 13.50 |
| | THE FORGER (USA: THE CLEVER ONE) | 6.99 | 12.95 | 19.95 | 13.50 |
| | THE FOUR JUST MEN | 6.99 | 12.95 | 19.95 | 13.50 |
| | FOUR SQUARE JANE | 6.99 | 12.95 | 19.95 | 13.50 |

ALL HOUSE OF STRATUS BOOKS ARE AVAILABLE FROM GOOD BOOKSHOPS
OR DIRECT FROM THE PUBLISHER:

Internet:   www.houseofstratus.com including synopses and features.

Email:   sales@houseofstratus.com
info@houseofstratus.com
(please quote author, title and credit card details.)

## OTHER TITLES BY EDGAR WALLACE AVAILABLE DIRECT
## FROM HOUSE OF STRATUS

| Quantity | | £ | $(US) | $(CAN) | € |
|---|---|---|---|---|---|
| | THE FOURTH PLAGUE | 6.99 | 12.95 | 19.95 | 13.50 |
| | THE FRIGHTENED LADY | 6.99 | 12.95 | 19.95 | 13.50 |
| | GOOD EVANS | 6.99 | 12.95 | 19.95 | 13.50 |
| | THE HAND OF POWER | 6.99 | 12.95 | 19.95 | 13.50 |
| | THE IRON GRIP | 6.99 | 12.95 | 19.95 | 13.50 |
| | THE JOKER *(USA: THE COLOSSUS)* | 6.99 | 12.95 | 19.95 | 13.50 |
| | THE JUST MEN OF CORDOVA | 6.99 | 12.95 | 19.95 | 13.50 |
| | THE LAW OF THE FOUR JUST MEN | 6.99 | 12.95 | 19.95 | 13.50 |
| | THE LONE HOUSE MYSTERY | 6.99 | 12.95 | 19.95 | 13.50 |
| | THE MAN WHO BOUGHT LONDON | 6.99 | 12.95 | 19.95 | 13.50 |
| | THE MAN WHO KNEW | 6.99 | 12.95 | 19.95 | 13.50 |
| | THE MAN WHO WAS NOBODY | 6.99 | 12.95 | 19.95 | 13.50 |
| | THE MIND OF MR J G REEDER | | | | |
| | *(USA: THE MURDER BOOK OF J G REEDER)* | 6.99 | 12.95 | 19.95 | 13.50 |
| | MORE EDUCATED EVANS | 6.99 | 12.95 | 19.95 | 13.50 |
| | MR J G REEDER RETURNS | | | | |
| | *(USA: MR REEDER RETURNS)* | 6.99 | 12.95 | 19.95 | 13.50 |
| | MR JUSTICE MAXELL | 6.99 | 12.95 | 19.95 | 13.50 |
| | RED ACES | 6.99 | 12.95 | 19.95 | 13.50 |
| | ROOM 13 | 6.99 | 12.95 | 19.95 | 13.50 |
| | SANDERS | 6.99 | 12.95 | 19.95 | 13.50 |
| | SANDERS OF THE RIVER | 6.99 | 12.95 | 19.95 | 13.50 |
| | THE SINISTER MAN | 6.99 | 12.95 | 19.95 | 13.50 |
| | THE SQUARE EMERALD | | | | |
| | *(USA: THE GIRL FROM SCOTLAND YARD)* | 6.99 | 12.95 | 19.95 | 13.50 |
| | THE THREE JUST MEN | 6.99 | 12.95 | 19.95 | 13.50 |
| | THE THREE OAK MYSTERY | 6.99 | 12.95 | 19.95 | 13.50 |
| | THE TRAITOR'S GATE | 6.99 | 12.95 | 19.95 | 13.50 |
| | WHEN THE GANGS CAME TO LONDON | 6.99 | 12.95 | 19.95 | 13.50 |

| | |
|---|---|
| Tel: | Order Line |
| | 0800 169 1780 (UK) |
| | 800 724 1100 (USA) |
| | International |
| | +44 (0) 1845 527700 (UK) |
| | +01    845 463 1100 (USA) |
| Fax: | +44 (0) 1845 527711 (UK) |
| | +01    845 463 0018 (USA) |
| | (please quote author, title and credit card details.) |
| Send to: | House of Stratus Sales Department |
| | Thirsk Industrial Park |
| | York Road, Thirsk |
| | North Yorkshire, YO7 3BX |
| | UK |

# PAYMENT

Please tick currency you wish to use:

☐ £ (Sterling)    ☐ $ (US)    ☐ $ (CAN)    ☐ € (Euros)

Allow for shipping costs charged per order plus an amount per book as set out in the tables below:

CURRENCY/DESTINATION

|  | £(Sterling) | $(US) | $(CAN) | € (Euros) |
|---|---|---|---|---|
| **Cost per order** | | | | |
| UK | 1.50 | 2.25 | 3.50 | 2.50 |
| Europe | 3.00 | 4.50 | 6.75 | 5.00 |
| North America | 3.00 | 3.50 | 5.25 | 5.00 |
| Rest of World | 3.00 | 4.50 | 6.75 | 5.00 |
| **Additional cost per book** | | | | |
| UK | 0.50 | 0.75 | 1.15 | 0.85 |
| Europe | 1.00 | 1.50 | 2.25 | 1.70 |
| North America | 1.00 | 1.00 | 1.50 | 1.70 |
| Rest of World | 1.50 | 2.25 | 3.50 | 3.00 |

PLEASE SEND CHEQUE OR INTERNATIONAL MONEY ORDER
payable to: HOUSE OF STRATUS LTD or HOUSE OF STRATUS INC. or card payment as indicated

STERLING EXAMPLE

Cost of book(s):...................... Example: 3 x books at £6.99 each: £20.97
Cost of order: ....................... Example: £1.50 (Delivery to UK address)
Additional cost per book:.............. Example: 3 x £0.50: £1.50
Order total including shipping:.......... Example: £23.97

## VISA, MASTERCARD, SWITCH, AMEX:

☐ ☐ ☐ ☐ ☐ ☐ ☐ ☐ ☐ ☐ ☐ ☐ ☐ ☐ ☐ ☐ ☐ ☐ ☐ ☐

Issue number (Switch only):

☐ ☐ ☐

Start Date:                    Expiry Date:

☐☐/ ☐☐                        ☐☐/ ☐☐

Signature: _____

NAME: _____

ADDRESS: _____

COUNTRY: _____

ZIP/POSTCODE: _____

Please allow 28 days for delivery. Despatch normally within 48 hours.

Prices subject to change without notice.
Please tick box if you do not wish to receive any additional information. ☐

House of Stratus publishes many other titles in this genre; please check our website (**www.houseofstratus.com**) for more details.